(Ralewing)

"There are windfalls of dreams, there's a wolf in the stars/ And Life is a nymph who will never be thine/ With lily, germander, and sops in wine./ With sweet-brier, And bon-fire, And strawberry-wire, And columbine."
—Hope Mirrlees

FANTASTIQUE UNFETTERED

A PERIODICAL OF LIBERATED LITERATURE

#4 Winter 2011/ 2012

FANTASTIQUE UNFETTERED

Issue Four (Ralewing) ISBN: 978-0-9831709-6-9
An M-Brane Press Publication
Publisher: Christopher Fletcher

Managing/Fiction Editor, Layout: Brandon H. Bell |
Poetry Editor, Associate Editor: Alexandra Seidel |Art
& Design Consultant: M. S. Corley | Slush, Editorial
Assts.: William Wood, Jaym Gates | Contributing
Artists: Kirsty Greenwood, Luis Beltran

Fantastique Unfettered is published by M-Brane Press. Send
submissions to editors@fantastiqueunfettered.com. Find
guidelines on the website: www.fantastique-unfettered.com

Some content may not be appropriate for young readers or ideologues. Partake at your own risk.

Suggested Retail Price: 9.99. Actual prices may vary. Order via Amazon, Barnes &
Noble, and more.
Newstand distribution through Ingram, Baker & Talor, and more.

An old friend's voice...

Late in William Browning Spencer's *Zod Wallop*, two characters exchange these words:

> *"Is there something we must do? We have come here for a reason, certainly?"*
>
> *"Reasons and more reasons my Lord,"* Raymond said, nodding vigorously. *"We must do what all men must do. We must do our Best."*
>
> *Raymond and Harry, with Emily between them, stared out at the ocean until the wind rose and salt water flew at them and finally they turned and retraced their steps to the hotel.*
>
> *"I don't know if I'm up to my best,"* Harry said. *"I haven't felt tip-top for sometime."*

While these characters encounter fantastic creatures like ralewings and big pharma reps, the darkness haunting the edges of the book is a loss so small it should mean nothing in a universe so vast. Anyone who has lost a loved one understands how that lack will grow into the greatest darkness of all.

If loss coalesces into a singularity, one cannot help but plummet into its depths.

Strangely, fortuitously, this issue of Fantastique Unfettered has burgeoned into a theme of sorts. Along the way, Alexa and I thought we knew it, like a chance meeting with an old friend. *The atheist issue*, we called it, and later *the rationality issue*. But we were wrong. Death is the voice we kept reading.

Perhaps Its words are a duality. A choice offered for each to make, like the choice Harry Gainesborough faces in *Zod Wallop*. To do his Best, or not. Perhaps Its words represent a range of modalities, and ahead sprawl myriad paths between blind hope and nihilism.

Is it all a mockery? *Nobody gets out of here alive*, cue the guitar solo. Is there a reason for suffering? Or a meaning at all? Is there Truth? *Zod Wallop* is a book that participates in this discussion. It is a book I hold dear, and recommend any chance I get. Because it is a good book, and because it is both honest about our predicament, and suggests, as another author, Dan Simmons, expressed it, that *we must face the darkness with defiant eyes.* And sometimes, too, we have to let go. So we can live.

In the final analysis, perhaps Death and loss are not singularities to circle in fitful, degrading orbits, but facts to be reconciled. Because through that reconciliation—some might call it redemption—we find that life remains our homeland. Come on: we have some Death to do...

—Brandon H. Bell, Dec. 3rd, 2011

"We are all in the gutter,...

We are all in the gutter. In the darkness, smell of rot, with a loneliness and longing in us strong and acidic enough to eat our hearts whole, to dissolve our souls.

This is the place this issue started from, in more ways than just some sort of editorial choice of theme. Early in our submission period, we mentioned on the social networks that we would love to see LGBTQ themed stories and poems dealing with Shakespeare and/or his works, because elsewhere in the publishing world, quite the contrary had happened.

As Brandon says, just atheism or just reason—and those two seemed such easy, logical guiding stars—were not enough though.

And of course, along came Mistress Death.

...but some of us are looking at the stars." *(Oscar Wilde)*

Mistress Death, La Mort, or Neil Gaiman's "Lady on the Grey" is not that scythe swinging, scary skeleton dude. In *The Graveyard Book*, there is a chapter called *Danse Macabre*. In it the dead and the living meet to celebrate, to dance together, led by the "Lady on the Grey," Death Herself. But there is no fear, no bleakness there, no gutter of simmering rot. The living dancing together with all the generations before them—dead but not lost—it doesn't make you think of despair but of something deeper and grander in us that binds us together, keeps us grounded: humanity.

Might that be why this issue is our biggest yet? A cry for humanity answered in words from people who are looking at the stars, not those far above, but those within *one another*? Might that be why we decided to dedicate our sixth issue to Shakespeare, the Bard, himself, to *honor* his memory and *celebrate* works and people inspired by his words?

I hope you will find a humanity in here that tells you about death, but in doing so, also about life, about *living*. We can't promise you an easy or pleasant read though, for how should we show you stars without first giving you deepest night, the most pristine darkness you can imagine?

Better to light a candle than curse the darkness.

It is striking that match that matters most.

I invite you to turn the page...

—Alexa Seidel, December 3, 2011

Contents

Issue Four | Winter 2011/2012

Nonfiction

Poetry

Three Tales of the Devil's Wife

by
Carmen Lau

Herein, lies, pity, excuses...

1. Good Old Days

Many years ago, when I was not the Devil's wife, I was a human girl.

When I was a human girl I wrote love letters to myself. I drew bright red hearts in colored pencil, copied down my favorite poems and stuck them in the mailbox. I gave myself boxes of Red Hot candies on Valentine's Day. I would eat so many, my stomach would burn.

When I was a human girl I sewed my clothes out of old draperies my mother didn't want anymore. I had dresses of sheer blue cotton, gold faux-velvet, polka-dotted satin. I made the same dresses for my dolls. I tugged their dresses on and off, on and off. I liked to watch the cloth slip off their pale, stiff bodies and wonder if they looked vulgar or not. Sometimes I tore their dresses apart while they were still in them, hissing, "That'll show you!" or "You cannot resist me!" Once the dresses were completely torn, I'd apologize and apologize, but of course they couldn't

10

say anything back.

When I was a human girl my best friend and I would tie our jump ropes between trees and walk on them. Half the time the ropes broke or the knots untied themselves. Still, I liked the feel of falling. I liked how the grass bit into my palms and knees, and the hum of my bones being jarred when I fell. But what I liked best of all was the moment I felt the rope give and I knew I would fall, that frozen moment. And how my friend would cry, "Watch out!" with her hands flying to her flushed cheeks, her mouth wide open.

2. A Visitor

I found a young man in my house one day. He was in the oven.

"Why, that's not a very clever place to hide," I said. "What if I decide to bake you?"

"Please don't," he said, quaking in the oven.

I took him out by the scruff of his neck--for being the Devil's wife, I am no longer really human--and set him at the table.

"You're very lucky my husband isn't home yet," I said.

He said, "Will you help me? You look like a good person."

He told me all about his woes--something about a dying lover or a lover already dead, promises made and longings unfulfilled. Honestly, I have forgotten the details, but the crux of it was that he needed two coins that the Devil always kept in his pockets. I never knew of such coins.

I said, "Are you sure it is he who has them and not someone else?" and the young man said, "Yes, that is what the wise old man said, what the witch by the lake said, what the stone in my shoe said." I said it was nonsense, and he said, "No, I am positive they are in the Devil's pockets." In a moment of wanting to make a point, I threw him back in the oven. He banged and banged on the door but I did not let him out.

My husband came home and asked what the noise was, and I told him it must only be one of his headaches again. He settled in his chair and closed his eyes, and opened them again and said,

"No, dear, I am certain it's not my head."

I told him it must only be the sun thudding down the hills to its resting place for the night.

"That's not what it is," he said, rising from his chair. "Tell me what it is."

I told him it must only be the new baby in her crib chattering her teeth.

"She doesn't have teeth but fangs," he said. "Tell me what it is."

I closed my mouth then and went to bed. He went through the house searching in cupboards and under bureaus, but though my husband has good hearing he never knows where sounds come from. My children and I can cry and shout and he will never know it is we who are doing so. At last he gave up and joined me in bed. When I was sure he was asleep I looked through his pockets. Indeed there were two coins, square in shape and heavy as stones.

"God will catch up with me any day," the priest said. "And then I will never have a moment without him. If you hide me I will at least be able to enjoy a bit of respite."

I opened the oven and gave the weeping young man the coins. He did not thank me but ran straight out of the house. I have not seen him since or heard how his quest went. My husband never asks about the coins. I wonder if he forgot he ever had them, and how one could forget something so heavy.

3. Black Horse

"Dear," my husband said when he came through the door bedraggled and huffing. "You would not believe what happened."

"Who is that with you?" I said, setting down my knitting. For hanging onto his shirttails was a wide-eyed young priest, his face streaked with

11

blood, his black clothes white with dust.

My husband, upon seeing him, tore his shirt off and ran away. The priest gazed down at the singed shirt.

"I think you'd better leave," I said.

"No," the priest said, raising his hands imploringly. "Listen to my tale and take pity on me."

There, kneeling on the doorstep, he told me his tale.

The Virgin Mary had turned my husband into a black horse with the aid of a magic bridle and given him to this young priest. He had been instructed by God himself to build a church at the edge of the woods. For a while priest and horse labored obediently under the loving eye of the holy mother. As soon as she left to take care of other affairs, however, the priest, who for long years had been plagued by the mysteriously unrelenting love of God, hopped onto my husband's back and escaped into the woods. The two traveled for uncounted days and nights, their eyes peeled for the mouth of Hell, when one morning they saw on the horizon the steeple of the very church they had fled. The priest knew then that he was truly blessed by the infatuation of God and could not escape no matter how he tried to damn himself.

"Resign yourself to fate," my husband told him. "You will forever be loved and favored by him." He cajoled the priest into taking the bridle off, promising to try to help him when his powers were

restored. Upon release he fled as quickly as the wind itself, but the priest held onto his shirttails, and here he was, on my doorstep, as humble as any beggar.

"God will catch up with me any day," the priest said. "And then I will never have a moment without him. If you hide me I will at least be able to enjoy a bit of respite."

"Come in," I said, "and let me wash and feed you."

As I scrubbed his clothing and warmed up a plate of meatloaf, the priest asked me all manner of questions. Had I ever seen Heaven or Hell? Was I dead or alive? What was it like living with the Devil? Only one thing could I answer with any certainty.

"Living with my husband is at times like living with no one at all. He is always away, busy with his work."

"How I envy you," the priest said.

Since all of my husband's clothes were too large for the priest, I lent him one of my old dresses. What a funny figure he made in that froth of dusty white lace! For days we cleaned and cooked and mended together. At last he threw up his hands.

"How can you stand it?" he said. "The baby cries from morning 'til night no matter what you do to appease her. Clothes are dirtied and torn as soon as they have been cleaned and mended. Food vanishes as soon as it has been bought. Let us run away."

I thought about it. What he said was true.

"All right," I said.

We each packed a bundle of dresses and fruit. I confess I had forgotten entirely about the baby by the time we had done packing, so occupied was I with plans. We left. We traveled through hill and dale, country and city. We begged, played handmade flutes and sold jewelry constructed from leaves and floss. We slept under apple trees and in alleyways.

One afternoon, as we walked down a long country road from one town toward another, we met God. One minute he was not there and one minute he was. He was dressed in a black suit and smiling. He opened his arms and took the priest in them. In a puff, both vanished.

I made the tortuous journey back to my house, where the baby had fallen silent. I knelt at her crib and begged forgiveness.

"A mean black horse took your mother away," I said, but she would not turn to me. I watched her chest rise and fall with breath. I did not wish I had never left, but I cared for her in my own way. How could I explain this? I could say, "Everyone has her own tale to tell." But that is as much of an excuse as anything.

——————————————————

Binary
by
Mike Allen

Phoenix witch, warlock harlequin, bricked in their towers,
sealed in spires side by side in the nights
when the moon still rose.
Do any other souls remain to haunt
this city
       of buttresses that proffer no cathedrals to the sky,
       of bridges that grasp at empty air,
       of steeples that lean like wooden legs,
       of street-veins opened and long since dried?
The witch has forgotten.
The fiend no longer cares.

He knows her rhythms, the way women once knew the sea.
Flesh and ash and flesh again. He waits till the time is ripe,
spins a pole of dust and cobweb long enough to bridge
his ledge to hers, a second pole for balance, begins a slow dance
over the stone abyss, to find the weeping girl in her prison
and leave her weeping more.

She's left
messages to herself
many, many times before,
scratched words and pictographs
and hieroglyphs on the floor,
on the walls, painted them in blood,
etched them with white lances of fire.
Warnings, they are all warnings,
but she's never mastered the language
that lets her understand,
before she sees his slow walk over eternity,
the approach of his scythe-horned hat,

14

his lithe limbs climbing in the window,
what he will mean, what he will bring,
what he will teach.

He enacts
in years like days and days like years,
all equal in weight and balanced in his hands,
this same tightrope act, with subtle variation,
its newest iteration born of long practice,
casting fuel, pouring ignition,
forging hatred in the air
until she's found the will
to unmake herself again.

Her rage fills every room, ropes of shrieking flame,
bonfire tendrils that grow, thicken, shriek,
hungry serpents that flow and flood and seek—
he sets foot on the ledge. They find his feet,
blend seamless with the red of his leggings, his harlequin coat,
        his tongue compressed in a death's-head pinch of teeth.

        He bathes in the fire.
        He screams, but not from agony.
        He bathes in the fire, still emerges caked in filth.
        He bathes in the fire.

The Butterfly Collection of Miss Letitia Willoughby Forbes

by

Alma Alexander

Herein, a new kind of house...

The house on the corner of Fifth and Amaryllis was not a house. Not really. It was a mansion.

It was a small castle.

The "corner of Fifth and Amaryllis" was a little misleading, in fact, because the house stood on a tract of land which took up all of the south side of Amaryllis, all the way up to Sixth Avenue--and on the far side from Amaryllis street the grounds of this particular estate abutted onto a public park which gave onto Iris Street on the far side. So this house was the only house on that block, really.

Built of stone, it was set back from the street. A dark, shoulder-high, manicured hedge, kept trimmed and immaculate and absolutely impenetrable, hid most of the garden from sight--only two gaps were allowed in this, a wider one which opened onto a driveway which curved beside and behind the house (no street-facing blind garage door for this house--if there was a garage it was decorously out of sight),

18

and a narrower arch which bore a low wooden gate, always closed and latched, and which opened onto a stone-flagged walkway stretching from the sidewalk of Fifth Avenue to an imposing front door. The walkway was bordered on either side by rose bushes gnarled with venerable age and bearing blooms, seemingly regardless of season except in the deepest of mid-winter, of unusual size and richness of colour. The front door itself was set between two large bay windows in which lace curtains were always drawn, the only windows on the ground floor of the house on the front side, giving an impression of rooms of prodigious size within and beyond them. The second storey consisted of a row of Colonial sash windows painted white, gleaming against the dark stone--serried ranks of decorous bedrooms and boudoirs, no doubt. Above that, a third storey, mansard windows set into the dark roof, possibly servants' quarters in the days that gentry still had live-in servants as a matter of course--and for all anyone knew this house still had them.

Above and behind all of this, mysterious and improbable, a glass cupola rose over the heart of the house. It was built out of hexagonal panes, giving the cupola an air of being a diamond cut and carved by a master jeweller; on summer days the cupola glittered in the sunlight, both beautiful and somehow forbidding, as though it was whispering, through its reflected scintillae of light, *I am not for you. I am not for the likes of you.*

But also, for a certain class of man, an irresistible *I am yours, come and claim me.*

"So, there it is," Darius Green said, lounging on the other side of Amaryllis and leaning with a studied nonchalance against the fence of one of the more ordinary homes on that side of the street. He had changed his name, legally, years before--but although he might have been formally registered as Darius Green there was a lilt in his accent which still betrayed the boy who had once been Adario Verdi, a stow-away urchin new-come from the back streets of Napoli with little knowledge and ability other than cut-pursing and thieving, things he had dutifully practiced and improved on during his years in London. "The thing you would have me believe is the abandoned Willoughby Forbes mansion. Doesn't look very abandoned to me, Mick."

Mick O'Leary spat sideways out of the corner of his mouth. "Abandoned is as abandoned does," he said. "Her ladyship--Letitia, her name was, or Lucrezia, something like that--lit out almost a year ago for destinations unknown, hunting for her father who had been missing for a good couple of year before that. That was it when it came to family--her mother snuffed it years ago. So far as anyone can tell, nobody's actually *lived* in the place since. It's just been sitting there, locked down, just like you see it."

"Looks cared for," Darius said. "Somebody's living there."

"No live-in," Mick said. "A housekeeper type comes in once a week. A gardener is in there maybe twice a month or so, doing lawns, saying how-de-do to the topiaries, puttin' down fertilizer for those monster roses. 'S all."

"And how do you know that it isn't just empty inside? A hollow shell?"

"Nobody cares for a hollow shell like this thing's cared for," Mick said. "There's gotta be something worth picking. An' what's more I know what."

Darius raised an eyebrow. "Oh?"

"Papa Willoughby Forbes was a lappy... a lep...a leaping..."

Darius was tapping his foot impatiently, and Mick abandoned his attempts at high-faluting.

"He's a butterfly collector," he said at last, scowling. "I do believe that's where he went and vanished at, someplace exotic, chasin' more butterflies."

"A butterfly collector," Darius repeated. "So what are you planning on stealing--butterflies?"

"You don't got any idea how much them's worth," Mick said passionately.

19

Mick was certain that he would have felt rather strange climbing into one of those mahogany dining chairs--they felt as though they ought to either rise and serve him his dinner, or else eat him whole for theirs.

"I asked, I did, at the museum--the girl who sells tickets out front is a friend of mine, and she found out for me. Some of the rare butterflies are worth a flipping fortune."

"Uh huh," Darius said, unconvinced. "And how are you going to convince somebody that you own some rare butterfly from some tropic paradise?"

Mick smiled--and it was not a pleasant smile. "I can sell anything," he said, the words a statement of fact, not remotely braggadocio or hubris. "You just got to help me get my hands on it."

Darius bent his gaze on the mansion. "We'd better have a lot of time to look," he said. 'A house that size... and it could be anywhere..."

"Oh no, not anywhere," Mick said. His eyes glided upwards and Darius followed them until they lit on the glass cupola.

"Up there?" Darius said. "What makes you think so?"

"It's a greenhouse, innit?" Mick said. "A nice little hot house garden."

"Are you telling me we got to go chasing after these butterflies with nets? They're all loose up there?" Darius said, suddenly less eager to attempt to glean the Willoughby Forbes lepidopterist riches.

"Not *alive*," Mick said.

He was starting to sound insufferably smug, and Darius told him so--but something about the whole caper had caught Darius's sense of whimsy and if half of what Mick was saying was true, dammit, this might be rather more fun than most jobs he found himself involved in.

After he had vented his annoyance at the little Irishman, Darius settled back against the fence of the other house and crossed his arms, staring up at the dark mansion across the street.

"All right," he said, "I'm in."

Mick pumped his fist in the air, discreetly, in a brief display of triumph, and then controlled his enthusiasm, the consummate professional .

"I figured, two days from now would be good," he said. "The housekeeper-biddy comes in tomorrow--and then the gardener isn't due until the middle of next week. We have a window."

"I'll case it," Darius said. "Make it three days. I want to know everything I can about this place--and three days is cutting it pretty fine."

"But I've already spent weeks watching the place..."

"My way," Darius said calmly.

"Fine," Mick said, with a rush of annoyance. "I'll come get you..."

Darius pushed himself off the fence, tipped his hat at Mick as though they had just been two random blokes talking of nothing of consequence at all, and turned away, back up Amaryllis Street towards Sixth Avenue.

"I'll call *you*," Darius flung back over his shoulder. "And don't stick your nose above the parapet until then if you can help it. Disappear off the streets."

"Yes, *sir*," Mick said sarcastically, tipping his own hat in response--but he had done it to Darius's retreating back. Somehow it had all slipped from being his own grand idea to being controlled by Darius the Mastermind, in the space of a heartbeat. "Disappear," he muttered darkly. "Right. With my luck he'll just go it alone and cut me right out of it..."

But two nights later there was a quiet knock on Mick's door and when he opened up there was Darius, slouching with his hands in the pockets of his overcoat.

"Tonight," he said, without preamble, "if you're still up to it."

"Tonight? You mean right now?" Mick squawked, taken entirely by surprise.

Darius shrugged. "Now, or you're on your own. I'm out."

"All right, all right, let me get my coat," Mick grumbled, ducking back inside. It was the second week of September, and although the days were still warm with the remnants of August early mornings and evenings were harbingers of the October that was on its way.

"Something is strange inside that house, and that is the truth of it," Darius said quietly as the two of them made their quick and quiet way back to the corner of Fifth and Amaryllis.

"Eh...*inside*?" Mick said, faltering mid-step. "You've actually been inside?"

"That's what's strange," Darius said. "I actually took the trouble to look around--I watched your 'housekeeper biddy' when she arrived, and I actually knocked on the back door while she was there, pretending to be selling something--she told me smartly to get myself off the premises, to be sure, but before that I was able to see a few things--that garage in the back, that's a later addition to the house, it's wood not stone, and I could see that there was a door leading from the kitchen straight into that space. I could not see a lock on it, and there was only an old iron

21

padlock on the garage door, the work of minutes to deal with. So the next day, I did just that--the gardener wasn't due for another day or two anyway, the garage is out of sight of the street, and, well, it did occur to me that it was unlikely that nobody else had noticed these happy coincidences before you did, Mick. This isn't a house that's exactly... secured."

"So?"

"So it did occur to me that we might be wasting our time altogether," Darius murmured. "But then when I got inside... things got... weird. It's as though that house doesn't mind in the least that people get into it, or how they get into it. It does seem to have an opinion about people getting *out* though. Particularly if they are carrying something that belongs to the house. There was a fine little horse head statue that looked small enough to carry and valuable enough to matter--and I was going to take it as a souvenir--but I was given... a certain sense... of it not being advisable for me to try and remove it from the premises. Twice I found myself at the back door empty-handed with no clear memory of having put the horse statuette down--twice I found it back where I first saw it, gracing the mantel. And I knew, I clearly remembered, taking it down from that mantel and holding it in my hand. *Twice.* Second time it happened, I just looked at it, and

22

I left it there, where it was. And I went away empty-handed. And I never even went up the stairs to the upper floors at all. There the stairs were, going right up, starting right at the toes of my shoes, and yet somehow I never managed to set foot on them. I was in there for two hours according to my watch--and yet I do not remember two hours passing, nor what I did with them other than taking a horse head figurine from its place and putting it back twice. I think the house has been left well enough alone because it's simply... *guarded.*"

Mick, superstitious by nature, began to slow down, lagging behind Darius. "You mean... haunted?"

"Maybe it'll dilute for two men," Darius said. "Come on, you big baby, it didn't *hurt* me, whatever it was, and besides this whole caper was your idea anyway. I wouldn't know where to look for a butterfly collection nor what to do with one if I had it. And perhaps the spells and charms work only for horse heads and not rare butterflies."

Mick was of the sudden opinion that any such spells and charms might work on any unsanctioned hand which tried to lift things that the house knew belonged to it, rather than protecting individual objects--and he was now just as loath to penetrate this 'abandoned' mansion as he had been enthusiastic to do so only a few days before. But Darius seemed to have something to prove and Mick somehow found his unwilling feet had dragged him to the last place that he wanted to be, the gravelled drive that widened into a narrow courtyard around the back of the Willoughby Forbes mansion. He heard his own teeth chattering as Darius suddenly made a small light flare in a tiny hand-held lantern which Mick had not seen him carrying--he must have left it secreted here, against tonight's need.

"Hold this," Mathew said tersely. "Give me a little light, here."

Darius's fingers swiftly teased open the padlock on the barn or garage door, under the light that Mick shook down on his hands from the lantern trembling in Mick's own--this was the padlock with which Darius had already made the acquaintance of a few days before, by his own story, and had been merely put back in a semblance of wholeness, easily pulled apart again.

"Come on," Darius said, pushing the garage door open a crack. "Bring that light in, and stop looking like you'll run like a rabbit if I turn my back for one instant. This way. Careful, the floor's uneven, and there's a step before the door."

He said the last just as Mick stubbed a toe painfully against the riser of the step, and he mumbled a curse under his breath just as Darius laughed softly and said, "Yeah. That one. Now come on up,

the door's unlatched. Come inside."

Mick stepped over the threshold gingerly, as though he expected demonic voices to whisper maledictions into his ears as he did so--but he heard nothing other than a quiet creak as Darius pushed the door open and then the sound of soft footfalls on the blue and white tiles on the kitchen floor, revealed by a shaft of the lantern light. Mick paused, lifted the lantern, tried to squint at his surroundings, but Darius's impatient voice from the shadows made him tuck his head defensively between his shoulders as he took another step forward.

"It's just a kitchen. Nothing that interesting in here. Come on, we don't have all night."

Mick followed Darius out of the kitchen and into an ornately furnished dining room panelled in dark wood, porcelain plates and cups glinting in the lantern-light from behind glass-fronted cabinet doors. The dining room table was huge and solid, with enormous clawed feet, surrounded by eight chairs each of which looked like it weighed more than a couple of Micks put together. It did not seem possible that such things could have been brought here from someplace else; it would have taken a team of elephants to deliver them and dozens of burly, bare-chested, turbaned slaves to bring them inside. The furniture looked like it had been

23

hewn in place, right here, from some giant mahogany tree which had mistakenly sprouted from between cracks in the stone-flagged floor.

But Darius was uninterested in this room, too, at least for now. He was beckoning from the far doorway and Mick followed with the lantern.

"There," Darius said, once they had entered the main parlour. "On the mantel. The horse head. That's the one that wouldn't leave."

Mick brought the lantern closer and obediently examined the small sculpture, but an examination by lantern light brought forth no obvious curious properties.

"You want to try taking it again?" Mick said dubiously.

"Maybe later. Bring that thing. Come look at the stairs."

The stairwell to the upper storey, centered in the entrance hall so as to be viewed to best advantage from the front door which it faced, swept elegantly upward in a gleaming curve of polished wood, a narrow strip of lush oriental-patterned carpet runner fastened in the middle of the stairs by means of a thin brass rod holding the carpet flush against the bottom of every riser.

"Odd," Mick said as they padded to the bottom of the stairs.

"What is?"

"No dust covers on anything, like you'd expect in a house not lived in this

long. And no dust. Look at this floor. Look at the stairs. And you'd think that the trinkets like your horse head would have been put away, seein' as there ain't nobody here to actually set eyes on it-- and same with the china, in the dining room. It's all left... ready... as though the master's expected any moment..."

"Perhaps he is, for all you know," Darius said. "Maybe it's all been cleaned up for the triumphant return of the Willoughby Forbes family next week."

"Maybe," Mick said, unconvinced.

He came to the bottom of the stairs, fully intent on climbing them; it was a few moments later, apparently, that Darius said,

"Well? Aren't you going to go up?"

Mick found himself standing with his feet a respectful pace from the stairs, holding out his lantern.

"Oh, right," he said, and prepared to take that step forward.

A few moments later, Darius laughed softly.

"You see what I mean?"

Mick growled, deep in the back of his throat. "I'm beginnin' to think that this was a whole lot of a bad idea," he said sullenly.

"Ah, but I think I have it kind of figured," Darius said. "We both aimed for the center. For the carpet. But if I go off along the edge there..."

He padded up to the staircase and put a foot carefully on the couple of inches of polished bare wood between the center carpet and the edge of the stair. Nothing untoward happened, except that now, and it seemed miraculous to see under the circumstances, he was able to slowly and carefully climb the stair.

"So long as I touch only this part of the stair, and neither the carpet nor the banister," Darius said. "It was like somebody had a blind spot--someone who only saw one person climbing the stair, and that person did it sweeping up the middle of the stairwell with one arm on the banister--just like you and I would do it if left to our own devices-- and assumed that that was the only way to do it. So carpet and banister were drenched in the 'do not go here' suggestion. Nobody was seen skulking on the wooden part of the stair and so it was simply... not seen."

"Such nonsense," Mick said.

"Come on, trust me. Don't touch the carpet, don't touch the rail, and you'll be just fine. Try it."

Against his own better instincts at this point, Mick did, and found that Darius was completely correct. Placing his feet with great care squarely in the bare-wood gap between carpet and stair edge, he was able to climb very slowly and warily, his balance oddly precarious given the need to also hold up the lantern so that it gave out useful light. He wound up doing most of that long twisting stair on the balls of his feet, and his calves were aching with the strain by the time he stepped out on the first landing.

He sucked in his breath as he stepped up on the last wooden gap, and saw Darius standing in the second floor corridor, squarely in the middle of the carpet runner laid there. Darius laughed softly as the lantern light illumined Mick's stricken face.

"No, apparently the carpet hasn't all been hexed," Darius said. "This particular one doesn't make want to march back down there in a hurry. Looks like once you're up here at least the first round of the booby traps is sprung."

"And what's up here?" Mick asked.

"We'll find out, I am sure," Darius said. "Maybe even your butterflies."

"I'm not for sure certain they're worth enough for this," Mick muttered darkly, but lifted his lantern, took a deep breath, and stepped off the bare stair onto the hallway carpet.

Nothing remotely unusual happened, and he let out the breath he had been holding.

"Okay, then," Mick said, lowering the lantern a fraction and looking around into the deep shadows that surrounded the two of them on the landing. "What now? Door to door?"

"I think I'd rather like to take a look at that rooftop butterfly house of yours first," Darius said slowly. "These will all be here on our way back. Let's look for a second stair."

The second stair led off the far right-hand end of the second floor corridor, a wrought-iron spiral in a matte black that sucked in the lantern light and made it look like they climbed on shadows instead of solid treads, but other than that it was free of the sort of enchantments that barred the entrance to the main stairwell in the hall. They climbed slowly and carefully, and at the top of the stair emerged through an archway into a little tiled anteroom which in its turn opened out into another corridor, narrower than the one below but still covered in a plain and utilitarian runner rug along its length. It was very dark; in the pool of lantern-light they could see wall sconces where lamps or other lighting fixtures used to be, but were no longer. The guttering lantern was the only light they had.

A number of undistinguished and very ordinary doors opened on the one side of the corridor, the side that faced to the front of the house--these would no doubt be the rooms behind the mansard windows visible from the street. On the other side, there was only one door--a big double door that looked like it was made of solid oak, held by wrought-iron hinges--the kind of door that looked as though it was built to stand up to a battering ram, oddly incongruous facing out into this narrow corridor.

Only a few steps beyond, the corridor ended in a bare wall, its length less than half of the corridor below.

"What a very odd arrangement." Darius murmured. "That door--it must open inwards, those wings are almost the width of this corridor, if you opened it out you'd be stuck inside the doors like a cage. A very strange thing to install up here."

Mick caught himself thinking that the doors were alike in some fundamental way to the massive dining room furniture downstairs--both looking as though they had blossomed into their final shapes here, inside the house, growing into their form and function rather than having been brought in or built into this structure by human hand.

Organic, kind of. *Alive.* Mick was certain that he would have felt rather strange climbing into one of those mahogany dining chairs--they felt as though they ought to either rise and serve him his dinner, or else eat him whole for *theirs*. Here, he felt a distinct reluctance to lay his hand on those double doors. It was not the same 'do not touch' air from the stairwell in the hallway, but something... different... something... deeper.

Mick cleared his throat.

"Let's get out of here," he said.

Darius's teeth flashed in the lantern-light. "What, having gone this far? Some thief you make. No wonder you never did a big job on your own."

"I know when to run," Mick said, realising his teeth were beginning to chatter even though the corridor was not cold at all. "I know when the best thing to take with me from a job is me own skin."

"Your valuable skin notwithstanding, nothing ventured, nothing gained. I think what we might be looking for--and more besides--is right behind these doors. Skedaddle, if you must. But give me the lantern."

Mick considered the alternatives--following Darius into a place the very thought of which was beginning to actively frighten him, or making his way back downstairs through this eerie empty house in the dark down long empty corridors and two sets of stairs--and decided that at the very least he would not die alone. He clenched his teeth, locking his chattering jaw.

"Go on, then," he managed to squeeze through the gap between his two front teeth, lifting the lantern higher. "I'm right behind you."

He saw Darius's eyebrow rise at that, but he said nothing, simply turned back to the double doors and laid his hand on the latch.

There had been no sign of an actual lock, and the door gave freely under the pressure of Darius's hand and swung inwards. Darius stepped through; Mick followed, with the light.

They found themselves in what amounted to another corridor--or, more precisely, more of a cloister, with its inside 'wall' nothing more than a series of archways leading through into the central atrium--which was the garden underneath the glass dome on the roof of the house. The moon was only a waning sliver that night but somehow the glass panes took what light there was and fractured it and focused it so that there seemed to be rather more moonlight in the garden than there should have been, and almost no further need for the lantern Mick carried.

While Mick gaped at the lush garden awash in magical moonlight, Darius was looking around with a more practical eye. He finally nudged Mick in the ribs.

"Over there," he said, pointing.

Mick followed the finger with his dazzled eyes, seeing nothing. "What?"

"Just follow me," Darius said. "Come on. Bring that thing."

They followed the open colonnade down to where it was closed off by a glass door. It was not locked, and Darius opened it and stepped into what looked like a large study, or a small library. A desk was tucked into one of the mansard windows that jutted out of the house roof; the walls surrounding it appeared to be built of books. Wherever there were not bookshelf-festooned walls, the rest of the place was a glass cage--the door through which they had entered, an identical door which led out of the study on the far end and presumably let into the cloister on the other side, and a double glass door which faced into the conservatory.

Mick had gone over to inspect the bookshelves, shading the lantern with his hand and keeping the light from the mansard window (it would not do for somebody from the street to see a burglar's light dancing in the window up here).

Darius had turned his back on the shelves and stood staring out into the garden, lit with that eerie bone-white light.

"I think I found our butterflies," Mick said in a low voice. "There's drawers down here underneath the shelves. And they're full of specimens."

"Damn the specimens," Darius said, without turning around. "They're out *there*. In the garden. Look."

"At *night*?" Mick said, as he turned to cross to the inward-facing glass door "That can't be right. Maybe they're moths..."

But they weren't moths.

Something had stirred up and disturbed what had looked like an empty and quiescent conservatory, and it was now full of fluttering shapes. The

28

set of the wings said butterfly, not moth, and even in the strange light the two of them could see that there was more colour out there than was generally known to occur in nocturnal moths.

"I'm going out to take a closer look," Darius said. His voice was strange, slow, almost slurred--as if he had been hypnotised, or enchanted, as though he was no longer acting guided by his own will.

Before Mick could formulate a response about how he had a very bad feeling about all this, Darius had pushed open the inner glass door and stepped out into the night garden. He did not close the door behind him.

"This is a bad idea," Mick muttered, setting the lantern down on the floor by his feet and reaching for the door.

"A very bad idea indeed," said another voice. Not Darius. Dry and high and leathery, an aged female voice. Somewhere in the garden right beside the open glass door.

Mick froze in mid-motion, his hand outstretched. *"Who's there?"*

A strange creature stepped into the light. It was shrouded, dressed in what looked like a beekeeper's outfit--throat-to-ankle robe; long gracile gloves reaching up to its elbows, with thin sensitive finger-sheaths which permitted easy manipulation of objects; a hat draped with a veil which rested in folds on its shoulders and breast. All in black. A black ghost in the bone-white garden.

Something tickled Mick's wrist, and he shook it off, instinctively; a beautiful butterfly with large dark wings rose and fluttered off into the garden. Two more followed it into the office through the half-open door, alighting on Mick's hair, his shoulder. He batted them off with his hands; one of them clung briefly to his finger with tiny, delicate butterfly feet before fluttering off. His finger stung where it had touched him. His wrist was beginning to throb, where the other had landed; looking down, Mick could see a discoloration starting to form there, like a dark bruise.

More of them fluttered in, swarmed around him. He backed away, swatting at them; from somewhere inside the garden he thought he heard a shouted curse, a cry, a low moan of pain.

"Darius?" Mick tried to shout in a whisper, but the name didn't carry very far.

"It's too late for your friend," the black ghost said. "It's too late for you too. They've tasted you. You might as well come out here with your friend or they'll break this glass door to get at you if you try to shut them out. And they can do it."

"Who are you? How do you know? What are these things?" Mick was panicking now, seriously panicking, and

the butterflies were everywhere. He had taken off his cap when they had come into the house, and now several of the butterflies had tangled into his hair. He tried pulling at them and yelped with pain as he appeared to try and pull out his own hair; they weren't letting go. When he brought his hands back down they were coated with a strange oily residue.

"Are you the housekeeper?" Mick said. "Get them off me--get them *off...*"

The black ghost reached down and removed the lantern before Mick could kick it over. Mick actually heard her voice break open into the dry husk of a laugh, a wry chuckle.

"Best thing in the world, if the whole thing went up in flames," she said, apparently to herself. "Best thing in the world. But they wouldn't let that happen anyway. Come out into the garden, do. It'll be a mess, cleaning out the study tomorrow. No, I am not the housekeeper." She paused, letting Mick try and figure out why there would be a mess in the study the next day and watching him come to the possibly exaggerated but largely correct conclusions. "Trust me when I tell you that it is already too late. They have you. They are mine. I know them. I made them. That is my sin, and I live with it. I am Letitia Willoughby Forbes and this... this is my butterfly collection."

29

The tiny butterfly feet were like acid on Mick's skin. His scalp was beginning to burn. One of the butterflies' wings had brushed across his face as it fluttered past, barely touching his cheek just underneath his right eye, and the eye had already started to swell shut--he could barely see through the slit any more. It hurt. It *hurt*.

Mick actually whimpered. "It feels like acid."

"It may be. They certainly added a few... refinements since I made them." The old woman was very calm, very matter-of-fact about it all--distant, even detached, as though all of it was an interesting problem that had nothing at all to do with her... even while she was taking ownership of it all.

"They're butterflies--they aren't wasps--how can they--"

"Oh, they're worse, they're much much worse. They're not stinging. They are feeding." Letitia's voice was calm, almost soothing, as though she were talking about something a million miles away and not right here, right now, trying to eat Mick alive.

Mick actually swatted one of the insects, hard, and it splayed against his shoulder where he had slapped it down awkwardly with one rapidly numbing hand. In the white light of the garden, he glanced over and thought he could see... tiny cogs and wheels, like delicate clockwork, instead of the smeared insect

flesh he was expecting. And as if to confirm his suspicions, the creature he thought he had killed shivered its wings after a moment, in an oddly awkward motion, like a broken clockwork toy. Then it actually managed to lift its badly damaged self and fly jerkily, listing to one side, back out into the garden.

"You can't kill them," Letitia said. "Not like that, at least. It's gone back to repair itself. It'll be back. Perhaps even tonight."

"What are these things?"

"I made them," Letitia said. "To prove something to my father. To prove something to my mother, who was already long gone and needed no proofs from me. To prove that I was better than either of them, alone. Instead, it turns out... Oh, *do* come out of there, there's a love. I really don't want the extra work, it'll be easier here in the garden."

Dazed with confusion and now pain, Mick finally obliged her and stepped out into the garden. He might have reconsidered, had he been in his normal mind, because a cloud of butterflies bore down on him the moment he stepped out into the white light, covered his arms, his torso, his head, his face. But Letitia had pulled the door closed behind him as he had left the little study and now he was out here, exposed, voraciously gnawed on.

30

He fell to one knee, then both, then to his hands and knees. His breathing was shallow, rapid.

"You made them?" he kept repeating. "You?"

"My father was walking in the country hedgerows one day and he saw a young barefoot girl singing a briar into a wall of full glorious pink roses," Letitia said, apparently to nobody at all, her voice oddly dreamy as though she were telling a fairy story to a child at bedtime. A story she knew well, that she had told many times before. "He fell in love with the magic of her, and he married her. But he was a scientist, and his world was made out of things fashioned from clockwork and brass and oil and steam; his dream was to fashion a creature every bit as good as man but unencumbered by the weight of a soul. Her world was spells and cantrips, herbs for healing and for mischief, songs and stories, the magic of the earth and the sky, the water and the garden and the growing things, like any good hedge witch's should be--her dream was to keep her spirit free, and her hands flowing with magic. They fell in love but they stood in each other's way--because she did not believe in life without a spirit, and he scorned and wished to shore up the fragility of life which depended on such non-empirical spirit to exist. So they loved each other, and they fought, and they had a child. Me.

And each tried to win me for their side of the war. So I learned at my father's side--there is a laboratory on the far side of this garden, he lacked for nothing there--how to make a creature out of cogs and wheels. He collected butterflies from all over the world, and I loved seeing his specimens so carefully laid out and meticulously annotated, but they were dead things in their glass cases, and so I made a clockwork butterfly, and another, and another, replicating his collection by mimicking the specimens in his cases. I learned from my mother down in the kitchen garden how to take one of these clockwork butterflies and somehow, while winding one up for the first time, give it the breath of life itself. I let them loose up here, in the roof garden, in the conservatory. And that's where they eventually killed my father."

"He never... went away..." Mick managed, his mouth almost full of butterflies, his lips burning with the gentle touch of their acid feet.

"He died in that very study behind you," Letitia said. "My mother had been gone for some time by then--she died when I was no older than seven or eight. Maybe nine. That was about the age I made my first butterfly. Mother is actually buried down in the garden--there's a grotto, with an angel. My father... we poured what was left of *him* out onto the rose beds that my mother

31

had loved. His ashes seemed to do them good. And after him, the rest..."

"Rest...?" Mick said. It was the last word he spoke, and his eyes, open under half a dozen butterflies each, no longer saw anything at all. But Letitia didn't appear to notice.

"The burglars who came for the easy pickings, just like you," she said dreamily, sitting cross-legged on the white-gravelled path in the conservatory, beside Mick's body. "I laid a few easy spells on the lower floor but they always found their way up here somehow. And their ashes went into the roses, some of them... and now, most go into the hedge of thorns. I'm growing it high, you know--high, and all around, closing in the pathway gate, and the driveway. We don't use those any more, anyway, we don't need them. And the house shall be surrounded by it, by a hedge of thorns that is going to be too high to climb and too thick to hack through. And perhaps in time they will forget about us, here in our little castle. And in a hundred years, two hundred, maybe the butterflies will have worn down, and worn out. And it will be safe again. And some day some hero will come hacking in with a blade, expecting to find a sleeping princess, maybe." She cackled to herself, softly, as butterflies landed on her and then fluttered off again defeated by her gloves and her veils. "Perhaps I shall still be sleeping,"

she murmured. "For them to find. Or perhaps there will only be a lot of dead butterflies, clockwork worn away by the centuries..."

She looked down at Mick one last time, to where he lay at her feet, not moving. Then she sighed, and struggled up, brushing butterflies off her arms and legs as she unfolded her frame, slowly and painfully.

"I have to remember to let the gardener know there will be fresh fertiliser next week," she muttered under her breath.

The roof garden was quiet, awash with ghostly white light, the only sound a susurrus of fluttering shadowy butterflies. Letitia made her way back into the cloister, back to the double doors, took meticulous care to brush off every last butterfly from her head and hands before she allowed herself to open the door and step out into the corridor, closing the door behind her.

"Did I do well, Mama? Did I do well, Papa?" she whispered, as she walked down the corridor, drifted town the iron stair, made her way down the wider corridor on the second floor to a white door on the far side of the house, and finally let herself into a bedroom furnished only with a single white-painted four-poster bed with red velvet curtains draped on its sides. Shedding her beekeeper costume like a chrysalis she emerged as a slender-limbed, fragile-built creature, white hair cropped short standing around her face like the halo of a dandelion puff, her eyes wide and dark blue, her mouth generous, her nose a little sharp but not unattractive. Long ago when she was young she might have made a passable sleeping princess in a castle behind high walls of thorn; now, she was just an old woman, moving with the slow dreamy motions of a memory of forgotten youth.

"Must remember... tell the gardener..." she murmured, as she climbed into the bed, laid down on it upon her back with her arms crossed over her chest and a small secret smile on her face. Her eyes closed, the smile lingering, her lips curving and parting to reveal tiny perfect teeth.

"Time to sleep now," a voice that was barely hers, barely audible, came from between those smiling lips like a ghost.

Above her head, as though they heard, the rustle of wings stilled as the butterflies settled back into the trees.

The big stone house on the corner of Fifth and Amaryllis was different from the rest of the houses which surrounded it.

The house on the corner of Fifth and Amaryllis was not a house. Not really. It was a place where a cloud of tiny, perfect, deadly butterflies made from brass clockwork and silk guarded the sleep of an aged princess waiting behind a hedge of thorns for a rescue that never came.

———————————————

ALEXA CHATS WITH...

BRENT WEEKS

AN INTERVIEW BY ALEXANDRA SEIDEL

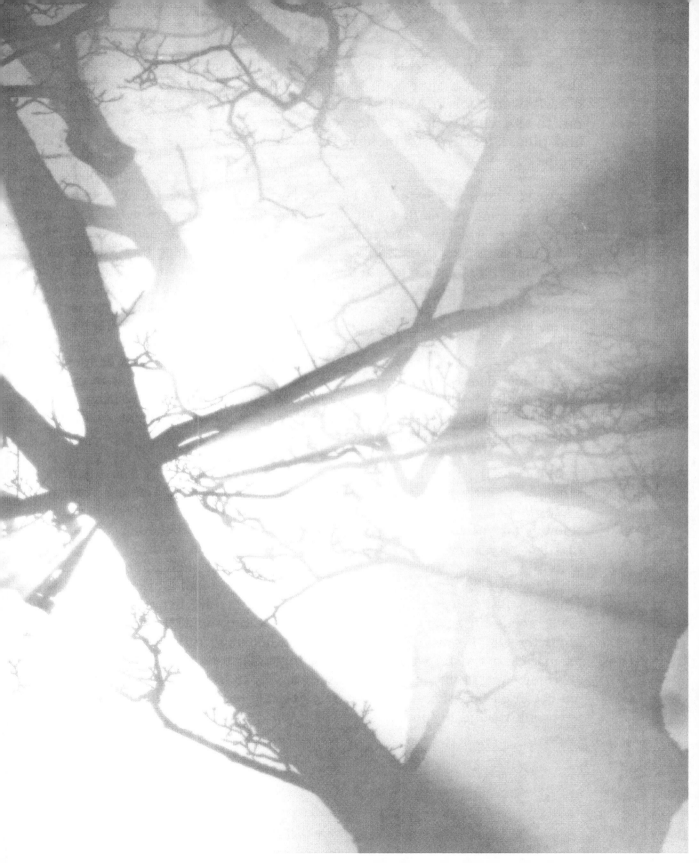

AS: Brent, in your bio you state that once upon a time, you tended bar. It would be neglectful of me not to ask what your specialty was, and please feel free to include the recipe.

BW: Well, this was a Montana bar, so you have to understand that a lot of the drinks were: whiskey. With a side of beer. And some Jack Daniels to wash it down. However, I did eventually find a pretty great Mai Thai recipe that I would make in a pint glass. Fortunately for my liver's sake, I have long since forgotten it.

AS: How does it feel to be a bestselling author? Did you imagine you would end up as one, back when you were writing things on bar napkins?

BW: I'm not gonna lie, it feels awesome. But mostly it feels awesome because it brings a small amount of stability and security to a profession that has very, very little of that. Most writers barely subsist. So getting to write for a living and know that next year I'll still be writing for a living, is really wonderful. I don't feel famous, as such, though. People don't recognize me in the grocery store or the airport or anything. And even though now I see my books on bookstands, I very rarely see people reading my books.

36

I didn't imagine that I would end up being a bestseller when I started writing. Honestly, my dream was simply to make a living doing what I love. I certainly wrote stories that were big and that were as good as I possibly could make them, but a thousand things can keep you from becoming a bestseller, and most of them are out of your control. So if I thought about it, it was more as a goal, something that I might work my way to after building up my audience for a couple of decades. Needless to say, it was a pleasant surprise to hit the bestseller list with my first book.

AS: When did you fall in love with fantasy, and at what point in your life did you realize that writing in this genre is what you want to do for a living?

BW: I was probably 8 or 9 years old when I first read Tolkien. And after that, I was toast. I really enjoy the life of the intellect, and the big minds that I got to interact with in college, and knowing that such communities frown on fantasy, I had a brief flirtation with writing literary fiction, and even tried to get into some MFA writing programs (although, secretly, my reason for wanting to get into an MFA program was simply to have the time to write, not to be told *how* to write). But even as I was applying to those programs, and reading all of the professor's works in the various programs, I got sick of all the pretension and posturing. It was odd to me that people who couldn't tell a story to save their life would sneer at those who could. So I decided to do what I love and do it as well as I could. In other words, I grew up and left literary fiction behind me.

AS: When I first read *The Way of Shadows*, the first thing I noticed was your extensive knowledge about weaponry, something the martial artist in me greatly appreciated. So, was it all "just" research or are you practicing a martial art yourself?

BW: I only have a few years of martial arts training under my (non-black) belt, so mostly this is the product of me faking it. Or to put it more kindly, a lifetime of research. That lifetime of research started when I got bigger than my brother who was 4 years older than me, and he enrolled in martial arts so as to be able to win our many fights. So if you want to count that as training, I suppose I have a lifetime's worth!

AS: In the course of the *Night Angel Trilogy*, you heap up quite a body count, writing the deaths of characters the reader has grown to care about. I'm guessing that as the author, you care about them yourself, so how

was it for you to end them with what is more often than not a violent death?

BW: Much like young men are much more eager to sign up to go to war, I think young writers are far more cavalier about killing off characters. When you talk to an experienced writer about killing off a main character, they start to think in terms of killing off their own franchise. If they kill a character everybody loves, they might be cutting off their own royalty stream. So I did what I had to. I guess that I was strangely fearless. The characters who die are characters that I'd planned to kill all along. I think I was also helped by having a level of confidence in my ability to create new characters that readers would care about. I didn't feel like if I killed this character that readers liked, I could never come up with somebody else that they would like just as much. I like to tell aspiring writers that one of the great things about this craft is that you as a human being will do so many things well, purely intuitively. All that said, when I make characters suffer whom I love, yes, it hurts me too. Azoth has to go through awful, awful stuff as a kid, and so do his friends. And it was no fun being in that dark place mentally. And when I let people die because they'd crossed the wrong people, I knew that was coming, because that's how the world works. But I didn't do it with glee.

AS: The people in your books never have it easy. You give out few lucky breaks. I don't really see the average Good Guy or villain either, but a lot of hard and relentless circumstances. Apart from not boring your readers, where does that come from?

BW: I think it's about consistency of vision. When you lay down the rules of a world that's gritty and corrupt, where the crime lords run most everything, and the authorities are ineffectual, or complicit, that's just not a world where there's going to be lots of lucky breaks. That's like telling a story about a street kid in the *favela* of Rio de Janeiro, winning the lottery and running around his neighborhood with the ticket in his hand, and not being robbed. When you start to throw in lottery tickets, you're just begging the reader to be pulled right out of your world and say, "Aw, come on!" So I certainly do believe in incorporating lucky breaks, but in my world, sometimes you'll have spectacularly bad luck, and probably the bad luck will happen more often than not, and then I think that lets me get away with the few instances of letting somebody else have incredibly good luck.

AS: Your writing, while often dark,

38

is not exclusively so. There is great humor in your books, but also a moving display of hope in *Beyond the Shadows*. Do you feel it is important to have both light and dark elements in your writing, and how do you balance them?

BW: The themes of light and darkness were very much on my mind as I wrote this series. And that's reflected explicitly in the titles of the books, which, while still obviously fantasy titles, do give a sense of progression from darkness to light. Part of my treatment of light and darkness comes purely from my own aesthetics. I don't like reading stories that are relentlessly dark and depressing. But part of this is also my own understanding of humanity. That is, guys in the trenches in WWI cracked jokes with each other. Amidst the most awful stuff you can imagine, people help each other out, or they laugh at the absurdity of something, if only to break the tension. And for as cruel as people can be to each other, I think there's great power in the little unexpected moments of grace. I think also having the full range of darkness, cynicism and nihilism all the way to hope, whether purely naïve or mature (and yet optimistic all the same), gives me the broadest possible palate from which to paint this story. It allows me to make the highs higher and the lows lower.

Or at least, that was my hope.

AS: In *The Black Prism* you have created a system of magic based on color, with the practitioner's irises as a visible manifestation of what color they can use, or draft. Where did that idea originate?

BW: I've talked a lot about the scientific side of my inspiration elsewhere, so here I'll say that I wanted to make a magic system with tangible, physical manifestations everywhere so you can tell who can use magic by looking at their eyes. Magic changes them over the course of their life. You can tell when somebody is currently drafting a color because it stains their skin that color. And when they throw a fireball, they have to be strong enough to lift it in the first place. The trick of taking magic and making it obey almost all the physical laws that we know, and yet stay wondrous and magical, was a harder one.

AS: Brent, what color is your magic?

BW: I have this color quiz on my website that's sort of fun, and I have readers ask me that frequently: "What color did you get?" The problem, of course, is that I wrote that quiz, and I know which answers mean what, and I know the formula behind how the quiz calculates which color is yours. If pressed to choose just one, I'd probably lie and say I'm a yellow!

AS: Which one of your characters is the most like you?

BW: For a writer like me, and probably for all writers (but I think particularly for a writer like me), whose greatest talent is making characters, this is an impossible question. Putting myself into these characters, understanding them as they understand themselves, imagining what I would do if I were under the stresses they're under, and if I had the influences on my past and the beliefs that they hold—this is what I do. So in some ways, when you ask which one's most like me, it's almost like asking which one was I most successful in writing? All of them draw from me, or draw from places I've been at various times in my life, or places I can imagine being. So of course, I've walked longest with the main characters, so I have a tighter bond with them, and I understand them better. But I deliberately make those characters *not* me. Kylar is very much me, but he's very different from me at the same time. Same for Kip, or Durzo, or Momma K. Or Gavin. This is the creative tension I live with.

AS: If you could be a character from one of your books, who would you be and why?

BW: Gavin Guile! He's got it pretty awesome. At least for a while.

AS: Is there anything in particular about your writing that you aren't quite satisfied with, that you still want to improve?

BW: Tons of things. I'm always trying harder and more things with every book I write. And of course, I always wish I wrote faster. Rather than answer the question now, I hope that in ten years, you can compare my most recent book with my earlier work and be able to tell.

AS: You have finished the second book in the *Lightbringer Series* not too long ago (an excerpt can be found on www.brentweeks.com.) How many more books are we looking forward to until the story you began telling in *The Black Prism* is concluded and have you thought about new projects after that? Apart from *Perfect Shadow,* will there be more books set in the *Night Angel* universe perhaps? There are so many things that are still unexplored after all.

BW: I believe I've been successful in wrestling The Lightbringer Series down to three books. I did have this great master plan where I would write one Night Angel novella in between each book of The Lightbringer Series. However, the last one, which was supposed to take me three weeks, instead took me more than two months. And when you're on deadlines, and writing really big books, that's two months you can't really spare, since I see my novel writing as my primary obligation. So in a month or so, I'm going to have to make a decision about writing another novella before I move on to the third, and I hope final, book of The Lightbringer Series, *The Blood Mirror.* I just haven't decided yet. However, I do know that when I'm finished with Lightbringer, I will be going back to tell more stories in Midcyru.

AS: Anything else that you would like to share with our readers?

BW: A little easter egg: If they read *Perfect Shadow,** which is set chronologically before The Night Angel Trilogy, but should be read after it, they will see a man who becomes Durzo's nemesis when he is just a child. Also, since doing an interview like this is ostensibly a marketing thing, I should mention that my agents' and editors' feedback on *The Blinding Knife* has been fantastic, and they think it's my best book yet.

AS: Thank you so much for taking the time to answer my questions, Brent!

BW: Thank you so much for interviewing me. I appreciate being introduced to your readers!

---

*For further information on how to get your digital copy, visit Brent's site www.brentweeks.com.

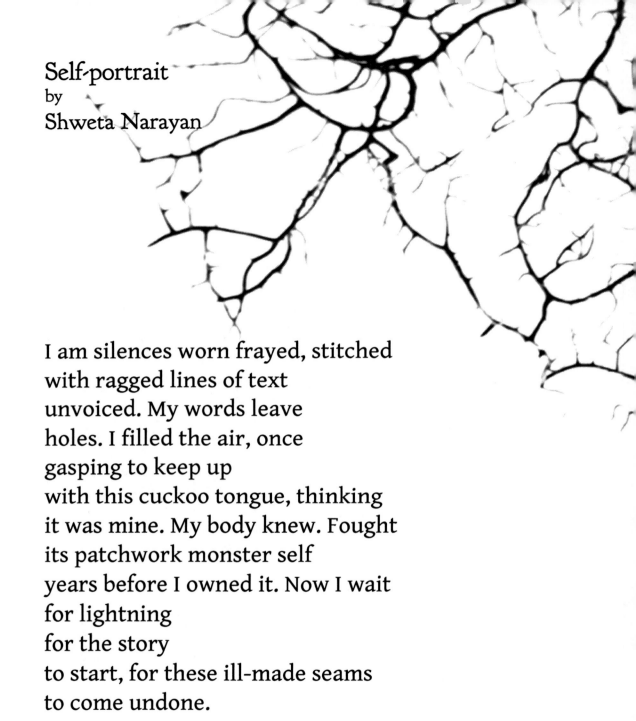

Self-portrait
by
Shweta Narayan

I am silences worn frayed, stitched
with ragged lines of text
unvoiced. My words leave
holes. I filled the air, once
gasping to keep up
with this cuckoo tongue, thinking
it was mine. My body knew. Fought
its patchwork monster self
years before I owned it. Now I wait
for lightning
for the story
to start, for these ill-made seams
to come undone.

Mr. White Umbrella

by
Georgina Bruce

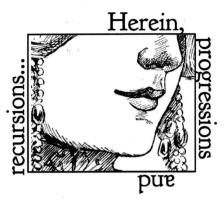

Herein, progressions... recursions... pure

Begin, my friend,
for you cannot,
you may be sure,
take your song,
which drives all things out of mind,
with you to the other world.
–William Carlos Williams

*L*ots of times... She sees him in the coffee shop, lots of times. He looks the same every time, exactly the same, as if not one atom of his body has shifted, not one cell has died. He wears the same leather shoes, and carries the same white umbrella. He always orders the same thing: iced tea with lemon. It comes with a small hard biscuit on the side of the saucer, which he eats slowly, nibbling around the edges, wearing it away. He looks young, but still too old for Kiko. She's only seventeen, but looks older because of all the pale make-up she wears to cover up her bad skin.

In rainy season, the coffee shop gets

46

pretty busy. Hot rain bounces off the pavements outside, sends customers streaming into the shop. Kiko serves drinks, takes orders in her meticulous schoolgirl script, places the biscuits to the side of the cup. She's not the best waitress in the world, but she isn't exactly trying. She's there for the money. At night she goes home to her one room apartment, eats a bowl of noodles while reading her Guitar Bitch and Mizz Shredder magazines, and despite being broke, she puts most of her wages away in a box under the sink, labelled 'Apocalypse.'

The Apocalypse is the evillest guitar money can buy, and Kiko is planning to own one someday. Kiko's got a boyfriend, a drummer, but she's deep in love with that guitar. She's got a song she's saving for when she gets her hands on that axe, and she hums it to herself as she works. That song is always in her head. Her soundtrack.

For a long time, the man in the coffee shop seems not to notice her at all. He sips his tea, chews his little biscuit, and watches the rain smashing the streets, washing into the stiletto heels of office workers, spreading black stains up their nylon tights, soaking into their trouser legs. Then the rain gets heavier, blurring the scenes outside, and the man turns back into the room and looks at Kiko. It's a look she hasn't seen before, or perhaps she has seen it but not understood. It is not merely desire, which is anyway familiar to her, but something else. Something hard, like resolve.

When he gets up and leaves the coffee shop, Kiko hurries over to his table. Resting on the saucer is a ten thousand yen note, and a business card. She picks up the card, turns it over in her fingers. It's matt black and its raised characters spell out the name of a place: the Crocodile Bar.

*S*ome time... The problem with Kiko is she thinks she's some kind of a hero, with her big spiky black pigtails, enormous desert boots and stripey Alice tights. Her skin is painted white and her eyes are crazy, covered with black eyeliner and purple bruises, her mouth slashed with red lipstick, like a slap round the face.

She drives the black Nissan Parallax, too fast, through the wet, gloomed-out streets. The front of the car is concertinaed, crunched up to the windscreen, and the doors are jammed shut. When she stops in the underground car park, she has to climb out of the window.

And then she gets her gun from out of the boot.

Death's too good for him, she thinks. But what the hell. It's all she's got.

*O*ne time... The three of them, two boys and Kiko, drive to the beach in the black Parallax, Jun driving, with one arm stretched around Kiko in the girlfriend seat, and Yoshi (bass, keyboards) in the back with his shades on, ear pressed to the speaker, because Jun's dad won't install a decent sound system in the car, and they can't get it loud enough to suit them. It's pretty loud anyway, blasting a sing called 'Shut Up and Explode' into their ears. All of them are singing along, as loud as they can, the windows rolled down. Kiko sings loudest of all.

They park next to the sea wall, and stay in the car for the end of the track. Yoshi shouts up from the back of the car, "Head on fire, man! I love this tune!" He leans forward and kisses Kiko on the cheek, and she grins and pushes him away. She gets out of the car, slamming the door behind her.

Jun follows, running down the sand and putting his arms round her, kissing the side of her neck.

"Hey," he says. "What you doing?"

She shrugs. "Nothing much."

"What are you thinking about?"

Everything. Nothing. Things she remembers and things she forgets. She keeps forgetting the song. How does it go, how does it start? She doesn't want to tell Jun about the forgetting. For

47

some reason, forgetting the song makes her feel ashamed. It's her song, after all, her creation, and she's been writing it and re-writing it for as long as they can both remember.

"I had a bad dream," she says, in the end. That's true, isn't it? She dreamt a maze of paper screens that slid back to reveal more rooms, more screens, narrow tatami-floored corridors between screens, behind which silhouetted bodies moved or stayed still;

It's a piece of paper, scrunched into a ball, and on it, scribbled in blue biro are musical notes. Chords. That opening riff. Yes, that's it. The opening bars of the song she's been singing in her head all her life.

---

steps leading up and steps leading down; and rooms within rooms, from which the entire path seemed to start again. It was like an Escher drawing, paradoxical and dizzying. She can't shake off the creepy, haunted house feeling it has left her with.

"Poor you," says Jun. "You shouldn't sleep alone, you know. I could stay with you."

Kiko raises her eyebrows. Go on then. Say it.

"You know what, Kiko," he says, and

48

he looks like he's going to say a lot more, something he's been rehearsing, maybe, but before he can speak again, Yoshi charges him from behind, wrestling him down onto the sand.

"Come on baby, let's make love in the sand!" yells Yoshi, as Jun struggles to push him off, and Kiko, laughing, grabs Yoshi's trousers and yanks him backwards so he ends up sitting on the sand at her feet. Jun picks himself up, rubbing his hand over his hair as he walks off towards the waters edge.

"Hey!" calls Yoshi to his retreating back. "What's up dude?"

Kiko ruffles Yoshi's hair, and he leans back against her legs. "It's me," she says. "I keep pissing him off."

"Why?" asks Yoshi. "You on the rag or something?"

She kicks him, quite hard, and dodges out of reach, laughing at his expression.

Jun is lying on the sand, face up to the sun, when Kiko finds him. The sand is pale yellow, almost white, and the sea is invitingly golden blue. Almost perfect, except she can't escape the feeling that she's done all this before. Déjà vu. Or whatever this is: her brain losing the thread of narrative that makes time seem to go in one way and not round and round in an endless loop.

Kiko gets it a lot, especially when she's tired. She has it now, looking down at Jun, standing over him. He holds out his hands to her, so she can haul him to his feet.

"Loser," she says, getting right close up in his face. "Fucking waste of space."

"That's me," says Jun. "Total loser. Dunno why you bother with me."

"Oh, mainly because you've got a car."

"That's what I thought. Heartless mercenary." He grabs the zippers on her leather jacket and pulls her closer.

"Heartless mercenary? That's a good name for a song." She hears herself say the words, the layered-over quality of déjà vu.

"You can write it," says Jun.

"I knew you were going to say that." Still feeling the intense familiarity, the feeling of being ahead of time, as Jun kisses her on the mouth. And she knows she is going to say it, but she says it anyway, "I love you."

But on the way back to town, they're listening to something by The Candy Spooky Theatre, and maybe it's the music, but she finds herself watching Jun, and seeing for the first time, not him, but something behind him. Like a shadow. She wants to touch it, and she reaches out her hand, but there is nothing there, only Jun. As real and solid as anything.

Another time... It is very quiet in the Crocodile Bar, which suits Kiko just fine. She'll make some noise. She kicks the door shut behind her, but it won't slam. It's one of those heavy, weighted doors that are designed to move slowly, in silence. No matter. She's going to get her satisfaction in here, one way or another.

The lobby is small, marble steps leading down onto the floor, six tatami mats enclosed by creamy paper screens. A squat ceramic pot stands in the corner of the room, and in it stands a single white umbrella. Otherwise, the room is undecorated. A faint sound, a scraping, alerts Kiko to an approaching figure, a silhouetted body behind one of the screens. The shape is growing, getting larger as it approaches, becoming more defined. Sharp spikes and aerials protrude from its head, and its body is ridged with hard angled shapes, like a stegosaurus. Kiko steps back into the shadow by the door, and the shape noiselessly slides back the screen and emerges as a waitress. She has on a stiff kimono tied in the Kyoto style, and her hair is decorated with combs and flowers and wooden ornaments.

She doesn't look at Kiko, which is probably a good thing, because Kiko is pointing a big loaded gun in the general

49

direction of the waitress's head, but she carries on through the lobby, opening the opposite screen and stepping across. Kiko waits for a count of twenty, then follows. Behind the screen is a long corridor of tatami and paper. The waitress is nowhere to be seen. Kiko tries to count her steps, but she becomes distracted by a growing feeling of disorientation.

The corridor intersects with other corridors at regular intervals. There are few markers to guide her. Each screen is the same, the paper of the same weight and shade. There is not even a scuff on the tatami. At the next turning, Kiko searches in the pocket of her leather jacket. She has the business card in there, and she drops it on the floor, and takes the left hand corridor. Three minutes later, there is another intersection, but it's not different at all. The card is there on the floor. She has come back the opposite way.

Take a different approach, thinks Kiko. She tries the screen door nearest to her. It opens into a small room, in which there is a leather sofa and a high table. On the table there is a jug of water, a glass, and a bowl of sticky rice sweets. There is something written on the water jug. She holds it up to the light. Etched into the glass, in fine delicate characters, the words: Drink Me.

Are you kidding me? She drops the

50

jug on the floor. It falls at her feet, and water darkens the tatami.

This time... After work she searches for the Crocodile Bar on her phone. It gives her directions to a spot in the middle of the city, a few kilometres distance from the cafe.

The instant she steps into the street she is soaked through to the skin, everywhere that the leather jacket doesn't cover. Her trousers cleave to her skin. People look at her like she's crazy, out in the rain with no umbrella. Whatever, thinks Kiko, staring down anyone who catches her eye. She ducks into the station, squeezes rainwater from her hair and consults her phone again. North exit. The short cut through the station brings another benefit: a red umbrella, neatly purloined from a bucket outside a shop. Kiko has many talents.

Out of the north exit, and Kiko puts up her new red umbrella. The rain is so heavy that she can hardly see past its metal spokes. Deeper into the city, everything gets busy. Taxis line up along the side of the pavements, and from a pachinko bar comes the crashing sound of money falling into slots. After about twenty minutes fast walking, Kiko is in the banking district. The phone directs her to a tall white building – an office block, looks like. There are several plaques on the side of the building, but one in matt black reads Crocodile Bar, in the same characters as the business card in her jacket pocket. She steps back into the street to get a good look up to the seventh floor, craning her neck and counting the floors. There is an open window up there. And something – no, someone – in the window, leaning out.

Something drops at Kiko's feet, bouncing a little off the tiles. It looks like a hailstone, but it's not. It's paper. Kiko snatches it up quickly before it gets too wet, and tucks the arm of the umbrella into her side so she can use both hands to investigate. It's a piece of paper, scrunched into a ball, and on it, scribbled in blue biro are musical notes. Chords. That opening riff. Yes, that's it. The opening bars of the song she's been singing in her head all her life.

This one time... There's a door at the end of a long corridor, a real door, not a paper one, but it's so small in the distance that Kiko wonders if she will ever make it there. Her steps don't seem to get her any closer to it, and she starts to believe that it is moving away from her at the exact pace that she is moving towards it.

Worse than this is the silence. Kiko has never heard anything like it. She holds her breath and swears she can hear her heartbeat, and then she hears something else: the silence in her own head. It buzzes faintly, like TV static. And the song she's been writing for The Apocalypse. It's gone. She panics then, scrabbling in her memory for the opening chords. How does it go? Her fingers cycle through imaginary chords in the air, and then, with a bolt of relief, she remembers the scrap of paper in her pocket. There it is.

Don't lose it. Don't forget who you are, what you came here to do. Don't get lost in here.

She sprints along the corridor, boots bouncing on the springy tatami. The creamy-white paper whirrs past her, and she runs faster than ever, hardly able to breathe, her stomach cramping. But she won't stop because the door is getting bigger, inching towards her, and if she can just keep running, she'll get there.

Some other time... Kiko wakes up early – too early – with a bad head, a head full of bad dreams, stuff she can't remember but makes her feel like shit all the same. And the song. Sometimes she isn't aware of it, it just plays behind her thoughts, informing the rhythm of her speech and her steps. And sometimes she forgets it, completely. It plays now, under the splash and patter of the rain. Without getting out of bed,

51

Kiko digs into the pocket of her jacket, discarded on the floor, and pulls out the scrap of paper with the notes on. Reaches into the other pocket, pulls out the business card. Connect the dots. But how?

It's still dark out, the rain drumming against the window. No sleep. She needs answers. She rolls across the bed, reaching out and opening the fridge, letting light spill into the room, grabbing a can of beer. It's so cold that steam rises off the metal. Breakfast.

She manages to find clothes with some wear left in them, decides yesterday's black eyeliner has smudged across her eyes in an attractive kind of way, hangs her head upside down and hairsprays the hell out of her hair. Fuck the ozone layer. It's way too early in the morning for any serious cosmetic labour, but Kiko wouldn't be Kiko if she didn't give it a little something.

The sky is fading to grey when she leaves her apartment block and heads towards downtown, her white sneakers glowing in the shadows. There's an NTT phone on the next street, wedged between a beer vending machine and one selling hot cans of coffee, and Kiko stops there, plunges in a phone card and dials the number of the Crocodile Bar. She gets a ringing tone, but no answer. After three rings the phone goes dead.

"Hello?" she says, "hello? Is anyone there?" But only the wind whispers

52

along the line. She tries again. This time, nothing. It doesn't even ring. Redial. After a moment's silence a recorded message: number not available. The automated voice is shrill and robotic, full of apologies.

Kiko puts the phone down. She steps back from the phone booth, trying and failing to make any decisions, buys a can of boiling Nescafe from the vending machine and cracks it open. Then tries again. After three rings, it dies. Come on, come on, redialling and waiting. But now she can't even get a ring tone. Fuck it. She slams the phone against the casing, angry now, only stopping when she clocks a car sweeping around the corner. Quickly she drops the phone, walks away from the booth. The car slows down alongside her, and she glances across. Tinted windows. Not cops, then. She walks faster, but the car keeps pace with her.

"Fuck you!" She breaks into a run.

The car speeds up, swerves to a stop in front of her, and two men get out. Two ugly fuckers, short and stocky with identical faces. They are so exactly alike that it is sinister, and Kiko instinctively looks for anything to tell them apart, but there is nothing. Tweedledum and Tweedledee. One of them (Dum, she decides) lunges at her, but she's ready. She flings the hot can of coffee in his face, forcing him back. Dee grabs her from behind, locking her arms down.

She stamps on his foot, kicks back and scrapes her heel down his shin, and he staggers away, shouting in pain, but then Dum is in her face again, this time flashing a silver knife, and he pushes her up against the wall.

Kiko spits in his face.

"You little bitch." He punches her in the stomach, hard, winding her, then pushes the knife up to her throat.

"All right," says Dee. "Take it easy. Don't kill her."

Kiko gasps, pulling as much oxygen into her lungs as she can. "You losers," she hisses. "What's up? Scared of a little murder? Chickenshit bastards."

For an answer, Dum punches her again in the stomach, and when she doubles over, he knees her in the face. Blood pours out of her nose and puddles at her feet. Keep thinking, Kiko. But she's losing the thread of consciousness. No. Stay with us. Someone is speaking to her. Ahem. Someone is trying to get her attention. She forces herself to look up, and sees someone looking at her. She recognises him. It is Mr White Umbrella, sitting comfortably in the back of the car.

"Nice to see you again, Kiko-chan," says Mr White Umbrella.

Kiko can't get the breath to speak, but she doesn't have to.

"Oh, this is nothing," says Mr White Umbrella. "Just a little fun. Just because I can."

She saves her breath and flips him the finger, but even this minimal gesture hurts, and she coughs, spitting blood onto the pavement. Mr White Umbrella laughs.

"Here," he says to Dum (or is it Dee?), "Give her some water."

The thug holds a bottle of water out to Kiko, and she smacks it out of his hand. She can stand now, and she does so, holding onto the wall and bracing herself to kick back against Dee and Dum's assault. But Mr White Umbrella holds up his hand, and the men step away from her.

"That was brave, Kiko-chan. Some would say stupid. But I understand. Food and drink are... oh, symbolic, aren't they? You know, in the old stories, they said that if you ate or drank the food of the underworld, you had to stay there. It became a part of you, then, you see."

"Fuck. You."

"It's just a game, Kiko-chan. Don't take it so seriously. Just remember we made a deal."

"You shithead," Kiko says.

Mr White Umbrella laughs, hard. "You are such fun! I could do this forever, darling."

The window whirrs up smoothly, until Mr White Umbrella is gone, and Kiko's image, bloody and white, stares back at her from the black windows, then quietly departs as the car pulls away from the kerb.

"What game? What deal? What fucking deal?" Kiko stands in the road for a long time after the car has disappeared.

Keeping time... The door is tall and wooden and does not open. Kiko presses her eye to the keyhole, expecting, for some reason, to see the world outside. Instead there is just a room, and in the room, a table covered with a white cloth, and on top of that there is a telephone.

Although she cannot hear anything, Kiko has the feeling that the phone is ringing. It has the look of a ringing phone.

But she can't open the door. She throws herself at it, shoulder first, hoping to smash through the wood, but it doesn't budge. She gets the feeling that she is supposed to do something clever right about now, come up with some sort of ingenious plan. Fuck that. There's another answer and it's going to get her there a lot quicker than using her head. She takes the gun from the left side holster and shoots several holes in the door, blasting the lock out, and then she steps back and kicks the door down. It falls, smashing to pieces on the floor, and she steps over the ruined wood and walks towards the telephone.

She picks up the receiver and puts it

54

to her ear. But of course there is no-one, nothing there. Only the dead, empty space between her and the rest of the world. No. There is something in that space. She listens harder, trying to clear a place in her mind for the sounds. There it is, very faint but growing in the empty space. Her song.

Bad timing... Plenty of ways to get a computer to give up its secrets, if you know how to caress its codes, tweak its digits, insinuate yourself between its numbers. Kiko has the knowledge, but she can't get the machine to open up about the Crocodile Bar. Every time she gets anywhere near, the computer crashes. She's been in bed all day, rebooting, starting again. She isn't a patient girl, but she is stubborn, and she's smart. She doesn't believe in coincidences. If the computer crashes every time she gets near to the information she wants, that must mean something. If she gets the shit kicked out of her for getting close to the Crocodile Bar, that sure as hell means something, too. Something bad, she guesses.

But what? And where the hell is Jun? She's been calling him all day, leaving messages, but getting no answer. In the end she calls Yoshi, and demands he comes over, and brings alcohol with him. Yes, more alcohol. She's been drinking steadily all day, trying to numb the pain in her face, which is now sporting two black eyes, and she's drunk, and scared. Mostly, though, she's lonely. Getting beat up makes you feel more alone than just about anything.

Yoshi arrives within twenty minutes, bringing a six pack of Orion Southern Star beer, a bottle of Midori, and a vinyl copy of All Imperfect Love Song by World's End Girlfriend, which he puts on the record player.

"What happened to you?" he says, looking at Kiko's face for the first time. "What the hell?" He sits down on the bed next to her but she turns her head away. She doesn't want to cry in front of him, and the tears are pretty close to the surface.

"Where's Jun?" she asks.

"I dunno. Work, I guess. What's happened Kiko? Tell me."

Kiko throws off the covers, leans over and takes the alcohol out of the plastic bag. "Nothing. Forget it. Let's get wasted," she says, sniffing at the Midori, before finally settling on a beer. Yoshi blushes, trying not to look at her bare legs.

"You're not going to tell me? What the fuck, Ki?"

Kiko's face is wet with tears. She feels dread tugging at her stomach. Why so scared? That spooky haunted house feeling is shivering along her spine, adrenalin is firing through her veins,

and the alcohol is singing in there too.

"You know what, this is fucked up," says Kiko, through her tears.

Yoshi puts his hand on the side of her face, and she--oh, Kiko don't--she leans forward and kisses him on the mouth.

He doesn't stop her, and she doesn't stop him, even though she knows she should. The computer falls onto the floor and she pushes him back onto the bed. He slides his hand down, pushing his fingers into her underwear, and she catches her breath.

"Don't stop," she says, and he doesn't.

And then, of course, they should have expected it; anyone could have foretold it: the sound of the door opening.

They both look up at the same time. Yoshi acts first, quickly pulling his fingers out of her and wiping them on his jeans. He leaps off the bed towards Jun, who turns and runs from the room, while Kiko is still lying on the bed, her underwear twisted around her knees. Her brain has taken a photograph of Jun's face; the expression she's never seen there before. Oh god. Oh shit.

The sound of car doors slamming makes her get up. She goes to the window and steps out onto the balcony in time to see the black Parallax speeding away and Yoshi sprinting behind it, shouting for his friend.

Time after time... Kiko reloads the gun with ammunition. If she doesn't find him soon, she's going to just spray the whole place with bullets.

Someone laughs quietly, and Kiko turns to see Mr White Umbrella standing in the splintered doorway.

"Well then, Kiko-chan," he says.

He looks different here, and his voice sounds weaker, quieter than usual. It is shaky, like it belongs to someone much older. It unnerves her, but she doesn't show it. She raises the gun and aims it at Mr White Umbrella's chest.

"I think I'll just kill you," she says. "Any last requests?"

"No," says Mr White Umbrella, laughing again. "Kill me! Go on! See if you can."

"Think I won't do it?" Kiko smiles. She's itching to pull the trigger.

"Maybe you would," says Mr White Umbrella. "It would be a waste of bullets. But go ahead."

"Aw, you're no fun," says Kiko. And she squeezes the trigger. And again. And again.

End of time... It's rage that finally gets Kiko off the floor, where she has lain in silence for a million years. When something clicks, when she gets that her world has been turned inside out, like a

56

sock or a t-shirt or something equally insignificant: that's when she gets up. She doesn't choose to get up. Her body is just responding to the rage, which shoots through her limbs and stands her up on her feet.

Rage puts her in the shower, ties her hair in bunches. It's rage that draws big black smudged circles over her bruised eyes, that slashes red lipstick across her mouth; it's rage that dresses her like a hero.

And it is rage, animating her body, burning a path through her mind, that gives her a plan. And she needs a plan, something to hold on to and steer her course. Because otherwise, she can only think about her pain. Otherwise, she can only think about Jun. And when she thinks about Jun, she gets that photographic image of his face, the last time she saw him alive. His eyes big with disbelief and shock and something else. Contempt.

Turns out that the plan involves firepower. Weapons, yeah. Kiko gets on her knees and pulls out the box from under the sink in the tiny kitchenette. Not enough money for a really good guitar, but it'll get you a gun.

Looks like the apocalypse is coming, after all.

Out of time... "I see you haven't

worked this out yet, Kiko-chan. So, what do you know? Do you know, for instance, how time works?"

Kiko shrugs, trying to look cool. *Shit. Fucking Shit. Why isn't he dead? The bullets went straight to his heart.*

Mr White Umbrella smiles, leans against the wall and points his umbrella at her. "Not how you think. That's how time works. The problem with the past, for instance, is that it's happening as the same time as the present. The future too. Everything happens at the same time. Your trouble is that you believe so much that time only goes in one direction. If you could believe a little less, you might get what you want. And I do know what you want."

"I want you dead." *Maybe he hasn't got a heart. Maybe I should have shot him in the head.*

"Oh Kiko-chan. How funny you are. Listen: I can give you what you want. What you desire. It's easy."

Kiko nods. *All right. All right then, you shithead. I'm listening.*

"See how you shot me dead just now? That really happened. But I don't feel like dying today. So what to do, what to do? I just pluck the moment out of time. Just like a feather out of a bird. Pluck!" He makes a gesture with his fingers, and Kiko flinches. "It's easy when you know how. Interested?"

You got me. "And what would I have to do in return?"

"I knew you would be! Let's make a deal. I give you what you want. And you give me what I want."

"Which is what?"

"A little... a trifle, really," says Mr White Umbrella. He smiles and lowers his eyes, playing at being coy. "What it is, I would actually like... Well. I would like your song."

Kiko shakes her head, not saying no. "What song? My song? I don't get it. You want that?"

"Yes, yes, that's all. Just a little trifle, like I said. You give me the song from your head. And I'll give you... now what was it? Oh yes, your dead boyfriend. Deal? I think we've got a deal."

"Are you for real, Mister?"

"I don't want anyone else to have it. I don't want anyone to hear it. Not you, not your friends. You have to just forget it. Totally and forever. That's the deal."

"And you'll... bring him back?"

Mr White Umbrella smiles. "Exactly." He puts up his white umbrella and twirls it playfully over his head. "Let's do it now. Ready to shake on it?"

"What happens if I can't forget? What happens if I break the deal?"

Mr White Umbrella puts his face very close to Kiko's. "Then I get everything, Kiko-chan. I get your time. All of it--the past, the present, the future. Everything. It won't be very pleasant, I'm afraid. But you're not going to break the deal, are you?"

She shakes her head. Who gives a fuck about a song, anyway? She would have given him her eyes. She would give him anything, in return for what he's offering.

Mr White Umbrella spits in his hand and holds it out to her.

"That's gross, man," says Kiko.

"Well, a deal is a deal, you funny little thing. Got to do things properly, haven't we?"

They shake, and Kiko pulls her hand away, wiping it on her jacket.

"All right then." Mr White Umbrella turns his umbrella upside-down and gestures for her to step inside. She does so, sitting down awkwardly in the curve of fabric, and he spins her around, very fast. She grabs at the metal prongs as they spiral-blur in front of her eyes, but that makes her feel sick and she closes her eyes, and when she opens them, she is floating down a stream. It is very peaceful. It is very quiet. She cannot hear the music in her head any more. And it does feel like a loss, to be empty of the song. It's gone, and there are no echoes.

After a while--it could be a second or an hour, she cannot tell--the umbrella runs into the shallows, and lodges itself on a sandy bank. Kiko steps out, finding her feet on concrete, finding herself at door to her apartment. She lets herself in, looks around at the devastation of clothes and make up, the stains on the

floor where her nose wouldn't stop bleeding and the tears wouldn't stop running. She is too tired to properly consider any of these things right now. Exhaustion catches her and drags her down onto the bed and into a thick, dark sleep.

*T*he last time... It is very dark in the room when she awakes, feeling warm breath heating the skin of her neck, and arms wrapped around her.

"Are you having a bad dream?"

Kiko sits up in the dark, rubbing her hands over her face.

"It was a bad dream," she says. "Shit."

She is shaking. Jun pulls her back down onto the bed, pulls the covers around her.

"You ok? You want to talk about it?" asks Jun. But Kiko says nothing, only pulls his arms around her tighter.

She strokes his hair, his face. "It's going to be all right. Everything's going to be all right."

He sleeps in her arms, and she holds him for what seems like hours, listening to the rain coming down, until the dawn breaks and she can see the shapes of his face and she can hardly believe that she has done it, brought him back to her. The song is gone, now. Forever. It seems such a small price to pay. Almost nothing at all. She thinks about what Mr

White Umbrella said about their bargain, and how she must never ever sing her song again, how she must pluck it from her life, her mind, her very being. And her heart thuds to a stop in her chest.

No.

Because she has remembered the scrap of paper in her jacket pocket. The scrap of paper with the musical notes on it. The piece of paper she's been carrying around for weeks (forever?) with the opening chords of the song scrawled over it.

Get rid of it. Now. Do it now.

Peeling Jun away from her, unwrapping herself from him, she climbs out of bed and picks up her jacket, digs her hand into the pocket. It's there, the scrunched-up piece of paper. She doesn't dare to even look at it, just screws it up into a little ball. Opens the window and leans out as far as she can, and throws the piece of paper down, and away, watching it fall like a hailstone in the rain.

Watches it falling down, down... it lands at the feet of a girl with a bright red umbrella.

Every time... One moment the road is empty, the next there is a building, right there, right in the middle of it.

Jun tries to brake the car and swerve away, but he's going too fast, out of control on the wet road, rain battering the windshield, and he can't stop in time. The car spins around on the slick road and hops forward, its frame buckling as it smacks into the wall.

All the time... She sees him in the coffee shop, lots of times. He always looks the same, exactly the same, like not one atom of his face has shifted, not one cell in his body has died.

For a long time, he doesn't notice Kiko. He seems absorbed in watching the rain hitting the street. But when the rain gets heavier, blurring the scenes outside, he turns back to the room, and then he looks at her.

It's a look she hasn't seen before, or perhaps she has seen it but not understood.

———————————————————

'cubus
by
Dan Campbell

the eyes are all I have:
blue gems, sometimes green,
others naught but shadowed onyx,
or cabochons of amber
beneath narrowing lids.

they say, when a man looks
at me that way, that he is dark,
and tall, and handsome,
that he is all one would want
in a mate, a lover,
a devil with whom to play,

and this is good.

they say, when she meets
my feral gaze, that she is wanton,
and cruel, obsessed,
that her regard is fatal,
her love, possession,
my yearning, fey,

and that is bad.

but who hunts whom
in this dance?

I want.

and I will have.

they say, while I watch
them writhe, that I am tender,
that I yield when I ought
be firm, withhold
when I should pay.

and it is never quite enough.

their eyes are all I have:
succulent and sweet,
bitter rinds 'round cloying flesh,
desire devouring all
in a single, starving stare.

Azif

by
Lynne Jamneck

Herein, a sound*...

Lycosa fatifera.

I don't like insects. They scuttle and their hard bodies are too resistant. When you step on one, it makes a noise.

I'm an epigraphist at the *École du Louvre*. An auxiliary scientist. We all have something which fascinates us and inscriptions are mine. After six years I still haven't ever had the urge to return to England. Not seriously, at least. Sometimes I miss beer that is just beer for the sake of it. Nothing more, nothing less. Of course, Paris has its charms, and I still find a dangerous sense of excitement in dodging cars and angry Parisians at all hours of the day and night.

I like languages, but I love what lies undiscovered about them even more. People think that academics are dull, dry and lead uneventful lives. They're mostly right. We're as uneventful as everyone else.

My phone rang this morning at the crack of dawn. Phillipe Frugè was on the other end of line. I was surprised. Phillipe is the Head of Anthropology. A quiet man, unassuming and hard to approach. Every faculty at the *École* has its stories about Phillipe; that his research methods were controversial; that his wife left him for a Costa Rican playboy; that he used to be one of the world's best and brightest archaeologists but that a degenerative eye disease forced him off the plateaus and behind a desk. I wondered about the thick glasses he wore.

I was still drowsily dreaming when the phone rang. I had fallen asleep again after waking up at four a.m. The old story; the last vestiges of the come-and-go insomnia that has plagued me since college.

Phillipe's voice was noncommittal enough in his request to see me. That morning; as early as possible, he said. I agreed and he thanked me and my curiosity was piqued. Curiosity? Well, that must have been what it was. A new discovery—something *really new*? It would make a nice change from Greek vases, clay tablets and Roman gold.

My imagination entertained all sorts of possibilities, in the shower, getting dressed, and chewing through a bowl of muesli hastily followed down by hot coffee. Then I saw the calendar. It was Tuesday. Nothing exciting ever happened on a Tuesday.

"Insects?"

Phillipe wasn't a man known for his sense of humour. Another one of those faculty rumours—he didn't have one. But the way the lines on his face moved spoke of several emotions, and perhaps there was the trace of amusement after all. He sat opposite me now, at the business end of the heavy desk in his office.

I wondered why he didn't laugh more often. But already the seriousness had slipped back into Phillipe's expression. He folded his hands on the desk in front of him. "His name is Madhav Halabi. He's the curator of Etymology at the Paris Museum of Natural History."

"And he thinks insects can speak? Well, I guess, of course they can."

I had learned that refusing the French to smoke—even in a house that did not belong to them—was extremely uncouth. Sandrine lit her cigarette and I watched enviously as she blew the smoke from between her lips.

"Phillipe, you are going to have to explain this to me a bit better. What on earth can I contribute to a study of insects?"

His smile was somehow tired, but still real. So much for rumours. "Have I told you, Vivienne, how happy I am you are here?"

"Blatant flattery. This must be important."

"Don't believe all those rumours you hear about me. A real heart beats inside this chest."

My discomfort dissolved at his laugh. "I do mean it," he continued. You bring a different perspective from the usual. Old habits are hard to break, Vivienne. People find it difficult to look at things differently from within prisons."

"I've known him for a very long time. I wouldn't ask if I didn't hold him in the high regard that I do. I would not waste your time, Vivienne."

What could it hurt? When was the last time someone had actually asked me to do something because of an emotion—and I could plainly see it on Phillipe's face now, though what exactly he felt was hard to determine. Besides, I hadn't been to the National in months.

"Alright," I took the business card Phillipe handed me. "I will give him a call when I get home tonight."

"He asked me to tell you that he would be in his office all day today."

I left Phillipe's office and didn't bother to go upstairs. They tell you Parisians move at a different speed from the rest

65

of the world. It's true, but not in the way we've been told. If there's one thing my meeting with the Head of Anthropology had taught me, it's not to believe everything you're told.

The *Musée National d'Histoire Naturelle* have sites spread throughout France. Today I was going to its location at the *Jardin des Plantes* in the 5th arrondissement of Paris on the left bank of the Seine. This is a part of Paris I never get tired of. The Latin Quarter with its lively atmosphere, bolstered by bistros and students pouring from the *École Normale Supérieure*, the *Schola Cantorum de Paris* and the *Sorbonne*.

Halabi's office was in the National Museum's Gallery of Palaeontology and Comparative Anatomy building. Famous worldwide for its collection of fossil vertebrates, invertebrates and its enormous eighty-foot gallery made of stone and metal. The large windows allowed the serenity of natural light to soften the hard lines and textures of prehistoric life. It is quiet inside the gallery. This time of day students were either still sleeping or out in the cafes, trying to wake up over strong espresso.

An intuitive sense about functional architecture helped me find Halabi's office easily through a navigation of rabbit warren hallways. It was at the end of a long corridor, and the light behind the closed door was the only one visible

among the offices. I knocked.

Madhav Halabi was younger than I had anticipated. His dark hair curled into his neck and his equally dark eyes were bright despite the tell-tale signs of overwork. At some point the tie around his neck must have been properly tied, but now it hung limply and skewed to one side. His shirt looked like he had slept in it. Nothing unusual about that.

He grinned when he saw me and shook my hand effusively. "Please, call me Emile. My mother hates the name, but my father had insisted on the Western name the day I was born. And do come in; now that Phillipe has convinced you, I should not leave you standing in the hallway."

He called me 'Dr. Martin' before I was able to convince him to follow his own suggestion. Then he disappeared amidst excited half-sentences to get coffee.

The books on his desk were eclectic; linguistics, ancient and modern history, literature, palaeontology and etymology. A multidisciplinary approach to whatever it was his research entailed. I liked him already. But I still wondered what it all had to do with bugs, and I asked Emile when he returned with the coffee, while trying not to sound out loud what I couldn't help but think.

"It never hurts to consider other perspectives. Did Phillipe tell you why I was so anxious for us to meet?"

"He said you think that insects can

talk." His face was so open and honest that I made a concerted effort to not say something offensive. "Human language."

His smile became broader. His eyes laughed along. "You don't like insects, do you?"

"Admittedly, not that much."

"There's nothing wrong with that. People always think I am going to, I don't know, get mad or something when they tell me. I hate falafel." He laughed, and I couldn't help it. His enthusiasm was infectious.

He said, "Maybe you just don't trust them."

"Trust them?"

"All those impressive dinosaur skeletons in the museum galleries—big, lumbering beasts, all extinct. Yet, the insects are still here. Flies outlived the T-Rex."

"I wonder Emile, would a linguist not have been more helpful to you?"

"I'm sorry, have I upset you?"

"No, but I do wonder about my efficacy in this matter."

"To tell you the truth, I wondered about that, too. I mean", he hastily added, "about talking to a linguist. But they are a logical bunch. Ethnographers still retain a sense of wonder, some room for what has not yet been cobbled into a framework for understanding."

He was assuming an awful lot. I felt somehow cheated for having been lured in by his easy attitude.

"You'd better tell me what you think I can help you with, Emile."

He headed for the door. "Bring the coffee; best if I show you."

I ended up spending two hours in a dark and cold storage room that had been converted into a working laboratory, surrounded by insects too numerous to think about. I had asked him if it would be okay for me to record our conversation and he didn't seem to mind. I was somewhat surprised at the trust he put in me, seeing as we had just met. On the other hand, I couldn't really imagine that anyone would want to steal his research.

I got home late that afternoon. A late start to the day confuses the day; you run into people you usually manage to avoid, leading to conversations you can't get out of. Tuesdays may be uneventful, but time still runs like dry salt.

I poured a glass of wine and waited for my laptop to boot so I could transfer the recorded file from that morning. This would definitely not be first time I'd encountered strange research and I'm sure it would not be the last either. Insects and detached phrases in Halabi's light intonations had been drifting in and out of my mind the whole day. I queued the file and put my feet on the

67

couch.

There was a hard knock and a shuffling sound—the recorder being placed on the table between Halabi and myself.

- Over there is fine, Dr. Martin—Vivienne (a smile in the apology). Pardon me, I was one raised a terribly polite child.

- So was I, but 'Dr. Martin' sounds like I should be diagnosing you.

- Too late for that, I'm afraid.

- These tanks, are they all full of insects?

- Yes. These, along this wall are locusts. The others, along here, are different species of crickets, and these are katydids.

- And what's in this one?

- Amazonian tick beetles. They're much bigger than any of the others. Much harder to find, too.

- Any particular reason you work with these specific insects?

- We've tested hundreds of different insects before we found a reasonable group that resonate clicks at the same frequencies. It's easier getting a few species in smaller numbers than it is to maintain a big group of only one. As you can see, there are quite a few insects in this room.

- And by "click" you mean the sound they make?

- Yes. Over here is where we record the sound and measure the vibration em-

anating from the insect.

- It looks like a giant computer motherboard.

- That's what it is, basically. Sandrine built it—my research assistant.

- What are these flat things?

- Piezo microphones, contact microphones. They record sound and vibrations when an insect is placed onto it. The data is recorded and processed in this computer.

- Once the data has been processed, how is it represented?

- Let me show you.

A moment of silence followed, then the the sound of a keyboard. Feedback from speakers strained the recorder's microphone for an uncomfortable second. A strange yet familiar sound issued from the laptop's speakers. It sounded like static at first, but then became defined by tonal shifts and volume dips. The sound of the sun.

- Cicadas. We recorded them in Australia eight months ago. Hundreds of thousands, relaying one continuous frequency. When we got back to France we began isolating the different tonalities in the sound and overlaying them with other insects we have recorded.

The sound stopped. A different one started up, sounding like an old radio being tuned. I listened closely. There it was. Something, but surely, not words.

- Did you hear it, Dr. Martin?
- Hear what?
- Let me play it again. Listen.

It played again.

- Dr. Halabi, I'm not sure what it is you want me to hear.
- Emile, please. Listen again.
- I don't know –
- There—don't you hear it? The words?

The droning sound remained for a few more seconds then stopped abruptly. The file had stopped playing. I realised I had been holding my breath. My tongue felt dry from the wine but I resisted moderation and poured another glass. As I brought the glass to my lips I felt something on my neck. I swiped, but it was only the tail-end of the scarf I had been wearing all day.

Phillipe found me in my office the next morning. From the look on his face I could see he didn't want to ask, so I didn't make him. But I told him there wasn't anything I could help Halabi with.

"He'd probably be better off talking to an anthropologist. Many societies worshipped insects in some form. Cicadas were sacred to the Chinese."

"Thank you, Vivienne. I appreciate your efforts."

He was going to leave, but I had to ask. "Phillipe, does he really think that insects are talking to him?"

"I don't know." his shoulders slumped, and Phillipe ran a hand through his hair. "Emile was such a brilliant researcher."

"Was?"

"His brother died two years ago. He didn't take it well. I'm surprised that he's working. Perhaps it's the only way he knows to deal with what happened."

"I'm sorry I couldn't be of more help."

"You've been very generous, Vivienne." He managed a short smile and then he was gone. Half an hour later I had a meeting with an overworked student who complained about not being hard enough on himself. He walked out a few minutes later with an extension and I spent the rest of the morning looking up facts about insects.

I went home early and decided to make myself a proper dinner, something I hardly ever did any more. TV dinners in France were akin to English gourmet meals, and that was what most of my meals consisted of these days. That, and marvellous red French

69

wine.

I wasn't expecting company, but surprised myself for finding comfort in the knock as I was about to take the casserole out of the oven. The woman standing on the other side of the door was a stranger, decidedly French, even before she spoke, and seemed completely unsure of whether she should in fact say anything or turn around and run. She introduced herself as Sandrine. When I asked if she was Emile's assistant she nodded. When I asked if he knew she was here she said no. I made her come in for dinner.

We didn't talk about insects over the *pot-au-feu* for which, I think, we were both grateful. Sandrine had the same sleepless look I had seen in Halabi's eyes. She accepted the wine I offered, and after finishing the stew and a glass and a half of the Bordeaux, her shoulders were less tense and she stopped glancing at the front door.

"Phillipe said you would not mind," she said again, explaining her presence. It was the first thing she had said when I opened the door. I didn't, not really. There remained in my thoughts a lingering curiosity about Halabi, the sudden and unexpected effect he and his insects had left with me. I couldn't help, however, feeling slightly ambivalent about why Sandrine was sitting at my table.

"Do you mind if I smoke?"

70

I had learned that refusing the French to smoke—even in a house that did not belong to them—was extremely uncouth. Sandrine lit her cigarette and I watched enviously as she blew the smoke from between her lips.

"Emile is gone. He took all the research with him."

"I saw him this morning. How do you know he's gone?"

"He is always in the lab room. He never leaves. He hasn't paid rent in months anywhere else."

"Do you have copies of anything?"

"Not all of it. The work we've been doing the last two or three weeks... I was going to make duplicates this weekend."

I could see why she was upset. Bastard. He'd surface somewhere and take all the credit himself. But credit for what?

"Sandrine, what exactly were you researching?"

"I thought you said you met with him, this morning?"

"Yes, but Sandrine, I'm not entirely sure what to make of Dr. Halabi's research—the research you and he—"

"I don't want anything to do with the research. Not anymore. I guess, since you were the last one to see him, I was hoping that you might have some insight as to why he disappeared."

I understood now. It really wasn't the research Sandrine cared about. "I'm sorry. I only met him this morning. He seemed like a nice guy." It sounded like a silly thing to say but it was true enough. Emile Halabi, aside from his research, had seemed...normal.

Sandrine lit another cigarette. "Do you know what happened to his brother?"

"No."

"He died in the lead up to the protests in Tahrir Square. He and three others were shot by Egyptian militia. They left them in the street to die in their own blood and the blood of others. It took Emile five days to find him. When he did, his brother's body was covered in insects. He told me that they were holding him together. That they were talking to him." The cigarette in her hand shook as Sandrine tipped a long piece of ash. When she looked at me there were tears welling in her eyes. "He loved his brother very much."

After her revelation, Sandrine seemed eager to leave. A weight had been removed from her shoulders and she could move easier now. When she had gone I made myself listen again to the recording I had made in Halabi's work room. I listened to it three times, trying to find inflections in Emile's voice, some instance, a broken note that would make me feel better. But not even the wine could convince me. And I had a hard time falling asleep later as the crickets, a sound which had before lulled me to sleep, now seemingly tried to tell me something I did not yet understand.

---

*Azīf is an Arabic word. *The Hans Wehr Dictionary of Modern Written Arabic* translates its meaning as "whistling (of the wind); weird sound or noise."

Sisyphus Crawls
by
Mike Allen

Sisyphus crawls
toward the honeydew-sweet air,
toward shadows of clouds beneath the bright skies'
    undersphere,
and the hornets storm the towers of his head,
the windows of his eyes cave in,
the friezes etched beneath the dome of skull
crumble down his throat,
faces broken away.

Sisyphus crawls
toward leaves like soft sylph wings,
toward the poetry of bird and wind,
and his atmosphere becomes thick as water,
dense as deep abyss descent,
and his arms snap from the pressure,
fold in upon themselves and tear away,
spine splinters, ribs cleave in,
broken buttresses beneath
a violated undersea dome.

Sisyphus slithers
toward new rain like soft cool hands,
toward the chatter in shaded streets,
toward the rumpled warmth of home,
and the passage compresses
like gravity, like singularity,
twists him into pieces cell from cell,
stripped, flayed, pared
into coils of seared mourning,
trickle-streams of silent wail,
into weeping ash,
into less, and even less,
and smaller still.

And these motes,
flushed past all light,
begin their slow climb anew,
their rise toward reunion,
the underworld's laughingstock,
its phoenix toy, bonded
by the cruelest joke of all,
the single thought that never breaks its hold:
The gate never closes.
The gate never closes.
The gate is never closed.

Life is Suffering: The Writer's Point of View, Being a Discussion with Hal Duncan & Mike Allen

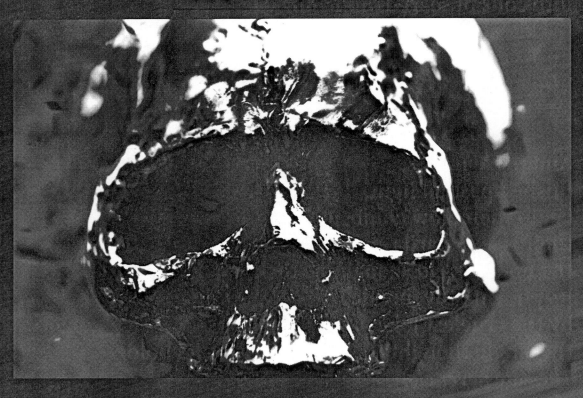

Conducted by Alexandra Seidel

AS: "Life is suffering" has become somewhat of a well-known Buddhist proverb (although it is actually more than just a proverb, namely one of the Four Noble Truths of Buddhist teaching.) It seems we all can relate to that sentiment; it's just one of these days, *life sucks.* You can't always get what you want, certainly not the cake and the devouring of the same, and so on.

This roundtable wants to explore the writer's perspective on *life is suffering*, or on *life sucks*, if you prefer the more pedestrian rendering. To start this off, I'd like to explore your thoughts on escapism, something that I'm sure reading is for most of us, but especially for those who make entire worlds up in their minds before they fasten them to the page (i.e. writers,) escapism must be a special talent. Hal and Mike, what are your experiences with the need to make up an *Elsewhere?*

MA: I've not done near as much "Elsewhere" manufacturing as Hal has—my first novel has only begun knocking furtively on agents' doors—but honestly, I'm hesitant to call what I come up with "escapism." Things tend to end badly for my heroes and heroines—their reality tends to be as frightening as ours, but in a different way, or even on top of the usual way. You could call it escapism in the sense that they present un-

likely situations, such as buttons that attach to your skin and unmake your flesh, or everyone in the world waking up soaked in blood that's not their own. These are "Elsewheres" in the sense that they fire my rather dark imagination, but I'd not call them escapes.

I enjoy a fair amount of reading that I'd consider escapist. I just don't seem inclined to write it.

HD: I'd echo Mike, actually. I've thrown together a few worldscapes where I guess you could subtract the story and have an exotic setting for any number of adventures, but I don't think of them as escapes. Even with the Kentigern of the Jack Flash sequences in *Vellum & Ink*—a luridly reimagined Glasgow with a Rookery and orgone-powered airships—the fact that it's based closely on Glasgow because I see Elsewhens as ways of engaging with this world rather than escaping it. Like, my version of Hell as a twisted New York is totally a fantasticated caricature of this world.

The idea of a need to make up Elsewhens for escapist purposes is actually... not me at all. As a kid, sure, I fantasised about being transported to Narnia, Barsoom, Dune, various wondrous ulterior realms, but it was always really about the adventure, not the worldscape. I drew a few ersatz maps, but from the start, my escapism was more about Jack climbing the beanstalk to steal from the giant, rather than the magical kingdom in the clouds in and of itself. With my first stories—those I made up to get to sleep at night—I built a recurrent character who might be a pirate in one story, a space cadet in another, not a realm. Vicarious adventure, yes. Worldbuilding, not so much.

I'd trace it back to one of the first books I really connected with being *The Borribles* by Michael de Larrabeiti, which kinda takes Peter Pan and scraps Neverland entirely. It's set in 1970s London, the Borribles being snot-nosed punk versions of the Lost Boys, latchkey kids turned runaway who've decided not to grow up. It puts the fantastic in a squat in London, which seems more truly liberating than exiling it to a Neverland. I mean, talking of "escape" via fiction seems... dubious. When Tolkien defends escapism in that quote about jailors and prison walls, I call shenanigans. If life is your cell, fiction isn't escape; it's a chat with other inmates, a workout in the exercise room, or maybe just a five finger shuffle in your bed. The only escape from life is death. Or there's liberation as freedom from shackles imposed by the screws—e.g. a mindset in which you submit passively to your lot but compensate by shooting up heroin in your cell, every fix of Neverland a temporary *refuge*. For me, fiction as a diversion is all well and good, but full-on escapism is the enemy of real freedom.

MA: Right, it's more about self-indulging, letting yourself be concerned with someone else's imaginary problems for a while, than any sort of escape. And a way of relating. I know that when I plumb someone else's visions of the disturbing, I tend to have two interrelated reactions: "Hey, here's someone else who gets how bad the world can be" and "Oooh, glad that didn't happened to me!" A lot of my writing aims in that direction.

I loved adventures in imaginary worlds as a kid, but it was the scarier intrusions, stuff by Lovecraft and Poe, Harlan Ellison's "I Have No Mouth and I Must Scream," Thomas M. Disch's "Descending," Clive Barker's *Books of Blood*, that left craters in my mind that I keep wanting to fill as an adult.

HD: Ooh, yes, Disch's "Descending"! Now there's a story that couldn't be less escapist. Shit, it's a nightmare of inescapable banality. What could be more miserably mundane than the tedious landing-by-landing descent of some guy—isn't he out buying a present for his wife or something, not out of love but as a complete chore, and stuck in debt while he's at it? So, going down the department store escalator, a moment such as that is like... the mind-numbing tedium of waiting for the fifth traffic light in a row to take forever to

77

change, when you're on your way into work at the weekend solely to pick up something you forgot to take home with you. It's an ordeal of passivity in service of a pointless errand. Disch nails exactly what it is about the mundane that can render it torture and just extends it, makes it his protagonist's existential Hell, taking it all the way to a final image that's more horrific than Orwell's "boot stamping on a face forever." Because it's not even significantly violent or lurid. It's the death of a thousand paper cuts, as grimly banal as everything leading horribly, inexorably towards it.

I wonder if it doesn't relate to Disch's scorn of wish-fulfillment in *The Dreams Our Stuff Is Made Of,* the way the whole New Wave is in an argument with the previous generation's technocratic fantasism, its tendency to render the imagined future another Neverland. It's sort of like he's grabbing the reader reared on refuge, grinding their face in the human condition. It's aggressive, brutal: "This is how it is, motherfucker; fucking deal with it, you fuck." I do think that sometimes the "life is shit" message of anti-escapist fiction can become... a depressive's refuge of fatalism, if that makes sense, a bitter insistence on futility. So I'm not really about that in my writing any more than I'm about consolation. But the hopelessness of "Descending" feels more targeted to

me. That disturbing vision is a tunnel vision, but it's focused on a particular *part* of life that's shit, and the sense of confronting that darkness is... I don't know, to me it agitates for action even if the story ends in the protagonist's utter defeat.

AS: Something Hal said earlier, life as your cell (or the mundane as torture,) and what Mike mentioned, writing from the perspective of someone who gets how bad the world can be, is actually one of the elements that I think can make writing interesting for the reader. As writers, what is your answer to that bleakness though? How do, how can your characters deal with it, if a simple escape alone doesn't work?

HD: To be honest, my answer to that bleakness—the idea that life is, when it comes down to it, a prison—is generally, "Fuck that shit." What I'm getting at above, with the notion of liberation from the shackles of mindset, is really, I guess, that I see that attitude as the real prison. I'm not a starry-eyed optimist, by any means—I do think life can suck in this respect or that; the world can be very bad indeed at times—but it's not some Phildickian Black Iron Prison where unless we can escape reality entirely, well, fuck knows what else we could possibly do! Not to me, anyway.

Leaving aside a small minority of psychopaths incapable of empathy, we're evolved such that life entails the *sharing* of suffering. For all our flaws, we do have a predisposition to minimise the suffering of others because we suffer with them. So life is more like a battlefield, I'd say, between that empathic impetus and the folly and weakness that acts against it, the cruelty engendered by the ongoing SNAFUs of the human condition. A large part of dealing with that shit is, I think, throwing off the chains of fatalism—that's assuming those chains are even there in the first place.

I mean, characters are always going to be engaged in a struggle on some front or other. Unless we're getting all experimental, it's not really narrative unless your protagonist is engaged in an *agon* on some level, a conflict—hence the term *protagonist.* How they deal with that, whether the resolution is positive or negative for them or their fictional environment, that depends wholly on the precise nature of the conflict and how it plays out. There's no reason at all to presume they must always already be dealing with some overwhelming existential futility written into the cosmos. In my writing they're more likely to be dealing with the specific problems of reality engendered by that outlook. That's pretty much the thrust of *Escape from Hell!* to be honest—that the absence of hope rests on the belief that hope is absent. The characters deal with that bleakness by, figuratively speaking, blowing it the fuck out of the way. They're faced with a system telling them their life is (eternal) suffering; they look it up and down, decide it's a crock, shoot it in the face, and walk away.

MA: Interesting how closely Hal and I seem to have dovetailed. My poem "The Strip Search," that won the Rhysling Award in 2006, imagines the Gate of Hell functioning like a metal detector at an airport, where inbound souls are systematically stripped of all hope. The twist comes at the end when the first-person narrator reveals he/she snuck some hope in after all: "I'm not going to tell you / where I hid it." That couplet cracks people up every time I perform that poem for an audience, and yet I think the poem remains so popular because of its underlying sentiment.

I do think I've delved pretty deeply into the bleakness. My short story "Her Acres of Pastoral Playground" that appeared in the anthology *Cthulhu's Reign* is about a man condemned to a different kind of hell, who has no escape from a truly horrific fate, and knows it; his struggle is all about making the good moments that are left to him last.

I wouldn't say, though, that I buy into the notion of life itself as a prison.

79

Fate is treacherous, yeah. Humankind is its own worst enemy, yes. People generally have the most to fear from other people, yes. But these things do not make for the sum of all life experience.

Sometimes it's the actions of the protagonists that bring about the bleakness, not anything innate to the environment. That's definitely the case in my Nebula nominee, "The Button Bin"—the hell the narrator ends up in at the end is one he tailor-made for himself. And yet, the journey, how he gets there, I wanted that to be eye-popping, mind-blowing, stomach-flipping. "Stolen Souls," the story reprinted in this issue, works along a similar dynamic. The hero earns his fate. In both stories, innocents are harmed along the way. One of the most unfortunate consequences of free will.

AS: Much of what you are saying reminds me of what I've read from the both of you, and not just the examples you gave. Looking at the writer's point of view as we are here, is there a certain philosophy in your writing, like the DNA of your story or novel, something that over and over in different ways addresses the same thing? As a reader of your work, I certainly have my own opinion, but I'm wondering how much of that is conscious?

MA: I'm not shooting for any specific philosophical point in anything I write,

80

though I suppose to some degree a reflection of my worldview in something I create is unavoidable. I've at times tried to write from perspectives that deliberately violate my own conventions and mores, but then, if I'm the one who thought up both the rules and how to break them, how successful can I really be?

HD: I do tend to be quite... confrontational, shall we say, in my writing a good deal of the time. I try to avoid didacticism, the story as vessel for moral message, because that's co-opting fiction to another purpose, making it mere means to an end. And even in the poetry, where it seems more natural to be directly articulating a personal philosophy, I've got at least one piece based on the fragments of Heraclitus and therefore happily arguing a perspective at odds with mine. But generally, yes, there's a definite stance.

Escape from Hell! is probably the most extreme example. Because it's using the action/adventure movie idiom in a sort of satiric attack on conventional mores, part of the fun is in the overblown spectacle of it all, just how far subtlety is thrown to the wind; it's philosophical belligerence ramped up to eleven, to the level of "How many fricking Nazis does Clint *kill* at the end of *Where Eagles Dare?*" There is an impulse toward metaphysical molotov-chucking you can likely see in most of my fiction, though I mostly try and balance it with contrary ethics. It's more interesting if a story is arguing with itself, exploring the tensions between philosophies, trying to resolve them via the narrative. I think fiction is partly, for me, a way of working out my stance, thinking ideas through with all this figurative malarkey.

AS: **Making fiction means to an end, that really nails it. My problem as a reader in these cases was always that I had no way of identifying with the main characters, and I'd think, well, it's nice, but I didn't *feel* anything. However, it was pretty clear that the author wanted to teach me something, was addressing me—the reader—more directly than other works that left me thinking and asking questions (some of which have made it onto the list of banned books.) When you write as the one who thought up the rules and how to break them, as you say, Mike, or as someone who tends to be confrontational as Hal says, to what degree do you have your readers in mind? And I don't just mean do you aim at a certain age group or something like that, but do you consider how readers may see themselves and the world around them, and how your fiction may fit into that?**

MA: I suppose this is where the arrogance of being an artist comes in. Because my answer would be: "No." I never think in terms of an audience when I write. And I would never claim to be able to look at something I've written and say, "Ooh! I know that this passage will affect everyone who reads it in X way" or "You stupid readers, I have something to teach you and you'd better listen up!" All I have to go on is whether the story stuttering out of me scares or moves or thrills *me*, and a hope that it will have the same effect on whomever else reads it.

One might say, this is what beta-readers are for, heh.

I will say that when I've tried to be confrontational in prose or poetry, I find I don't do it well... my words take on all the heavy-handedness and none of the energizing zeal. I think part of it has to do, too, that what seems to fire my imagination isn't sweeping injustice, though there's plenty of that to go around, but personal betrayals. Of course these can have larger implications, too, as my years as a crime reporter taught me. A courtroom shines a mercilessly bright light on the horrible things people who ostensibly love each other will do to one another behind closed doors.

HD: I'm always thinking about how people see themselves and the world

81

around them, to be honest—it's probably one of my central concerns, the idea that everyone has a personal semiocosm, a world of signs that's a sort of superposition of potential configurations, a worldview coded in the denotations and connotations, the relationships between them, the stories we've bought into already because they're implicit in that matrix. Like, if I've had a collie help me out of a burning building and you've watched a pitbull rip a child's throat out, the word dog likely has different imports to us. It might bind to *faithful* for me, *brutal* for you. Or to put it the other way round—if *dog* binds to *faithful* for me and *brutal* for you, my semiocosm has one story implicit in it, yours another. The dog is always already a creature that helps you out of a burning building and/or rips a child's throat out. That's what we mean by a story fitting in with a reader's worldview or not, I'd say.

Anyway, I'm interested in how narrative might stabilise or reconfigure a person's semiocosm, how a news story might entrench or revise what *dog* means to them. Think of how the last decade's news narratives have changed how the word *muslim* sits in many people's worldview, if you want a more pointed example. A profoundly negative import has been entrenched in many individual worldviews and in the gestalt semiocosm we call culture as a whole.

82

I'm interested in this shit—I sorta have to be—because similar entrenchment has gone on around words like *sodomite*. I'm all too aware of how my fiction might not fit in with a reader's personal semiocosm then.

That doesn't mean I'm going to *make it* fit in, of course. If a dog could write fiction, he's not going to write Kujo just to pander to a human audience brainwashed to hate and fear dogs by evil feline overlords. That would be one dumb dog, for all his literary skills. No, he's going to write for his fellow mutts and whelps, for all those beatniks and bleeding hearts among the humans—the *godless commie pinko cur-lovers* as those nefarious cats would have it. When it comes to readers with worldviews hostile to his ripping yarn of canine heroism, well, if they reject it on principle, so it goes, but with a little luck they'll run with it for the sake of a good story and come out the other end with their worldview opened up a little.

I see a corollary to what Mike said, I guess: that one can maybe look at a work and be sure a certain passage will affect a subset of people in X way—where X involves froth-mouthed loathing. You can be sure your fiction doesn't fit with some reader's worldview, that somebody will hate exactly what's right about it indeed, for you and your kindred spirits. And? Are you going to gut the story, turn it inside out, just to satisfy those naysayers, when you're only going to end up with a new set of haters—including *you yourself?*

MA: I certainly hope not. And shame on anyone who expects you to. (Unfortunately, that has to include quite a few in the industry. Rachel Manija Brown and Sherwood Smith went public not long ago with the revelation that agents were offering to represent their YA novel if they excised the gay character first.)

Earlier this year I wrote a short story, inspired by the art of Alessandro Bavari, in which I tried to build a world in which, among other things, gender is as adjustable and interchangeable as hair; something people can even choose to dispense with altogether and no one bats a surgically-altered eye. That story, called "Twa Sisters," hasn't found a taker yet—I admit I am curious what reaction there might be if any editor ever decides to give it a chance at an audience.

But this element of the story dealing with gender was for me more a side effect of exploring the world my brain built around Bavari's photo montages. It fascinated me enough that I've since written a poem set in the same milieu and started another short story, which ain't done yet because of the multitude of other distractions we writers face.

HD: Sounds cool. Funny enough, I have an unfinished novella that's going for a sort of "Ray Bradbury meets Guy Davenport meets Virgil" pastoral vibe, set on a far-future Mars that's all very Arcadian, where sexuality is measured in kinsey and hanker (preference and appetence), both entirely tweakable. (Gender would be too, although that's outside the frame.) Mid-range kinseys are the norm, to the extent that two kinsey "ones" are wryly amused when the main characters bring them together—like, "We're the only two heterosexuals they know. Clearly we must be perfect for each other."

Anyway, the whole story turns on an erastes/eromenos relationship the main characters throw themselves into; it's all very Eclogues. And as such... well, I'm guessing some readers will be squeamish about my equivalent of Virgil's shepherds. It's not like they're so young as to be dodgy—*that* aspect of Davenport I'll happily eschew—but the very point of the story is to explore an idea of the idyll that doesn't end with puberty, to have the carefree spirit of Huck Finn, the Neverland playfulness of the pastoral setting itself, persist in part because sex isn't a locus of angst in this world. The fruit isn't forbidden in this garden, so you get to play in it until *real* adult worries fuck it up for you. If readers don't get that though, it may just read like some creepy-ass twink porn.

But actually, that's a good example of how it applies to technique as well as substance, how you just have to do what works for you and hope the reader will connect with it. I suspect that more people will have problems with that story's dense textual approach than with what's going on in it. It's partially told from the viewpoint of the plants around the characters, with a ridiculous level of botanical vocabulary woven through it, not to mention a lexis of obscure if not downright obsolete archaicisms. It's absolutely inherent to the story, where the numinous animism of Arcadia is replicated by the richness of information, the level of science, history and cultural meaning attached even to a hyacinth flower, say, but it's the opposite of making allowances for the reader. I imagine a lot of readers asking what the fuck *sprack* means.

AS: Gentlemen, it seems like you are laying the groundwork for an anthology right here! I for one would be thrilled to read it.

But to conclude this little gathering, what is your reaction to *life is suffering* as writers, and do you think that being a writer makes you think about and react to stances like that differently from your ordinary day-jobber? If so, how?

MA: I *am* an ordinary day-jobber. For a long time my day job (well, really, my night job) was unloading freight from the backs of 18-wheelers in a department store. Then I landed the bottom-rung version of the job I have now, newspaper reporter, and I have to say, it opened up my world quite a bit. Earning my living became substantially less of a grind. And yet, a significant part of my job involved witnessing and recording the suffering of others. Without question terrible suffering visits people who've done nothing to invoke or provoke it. It's a theme I've tried to explore in my fiction writing as well, though it doesn't seem one that editors find terribly enticing, heh—though I think readers in general perhaps prefer that incidents in fiction be less random than in life.

HD: I'm full-time writing now, but I had a day-job for years, and I'm not sure I'd see a big difference in mindset between me then and me now—or between writers and "day-jobbers" in general. If anything, I look at my last day job—inhouse programmer for a thread-dyer—as more formative. That opened up my world in literal geographic terms. I had a few jaunts to foreign climes to install software in this factory or that—in small town North Carolina, Mexico, Romania, Turkey—and that sort of experience is just invaluable.

It's hard to explain, but going out with the locals you're working beside on

84

their Friday night in Orizaba, getting smashed in a bar as a rock band plays audience requests scribbled on slips of paper, where the people who speak English have adopted you so wholly as a mate that they start to forget you don't speak Spanish—the whole Lost in Translation experience only utterly comfortable—moments like that have had more impact on my worldview than just being someone who makes up stories, I think. It's about defamiliarisation, experiencing the deep structures of friendship because the surface structure of chat suddenly has no meaning. It's like turning down the vocal track on a song, the lead guitar too, and suddenly you hear this powerful bass riff underpinning everything, like a level of detail is removed so suddenly you see the basic architecture of this aspect of life.

Hell, that could well be part of why I don't see life as suffering. For me, with these glimpses of the familiar in the foreign, it's mostly been the familial and filial that jumped out, the interactions, the relationships, so when I think of life in the abstract, I think community, culture, what goes on *between* individual beings as much as what goes on within one individual taken in isolation.

MA: When I talk about earning my living becoming less of a grind, my world opening up, it's because my job allowed me to use my talents to contribute to the communities I'm part of. And that fed my creative writing in invaluable ways. Funny, how much we misanthropic writers can get out of human interaction.

HD: Indeed. I think that whatever my worldview, life would be fuel for the writing as much as anything else.

AS: That right there is just a beautiful note to end on. Thank you both for participating in this very first FU roundtable!

To find links to many of Mike's stories (and other Cool Stuff), go visit his online home at www. descentintolight.com.

An audio version of his poem "The Strip Search" can also be found there: http://descentintolight.com/2011/04/29/poems-from-the-journey-to-kailash-xii/

If podcasts are your thing, StarShipSofa offers two, featuring Mike Allen's very own vocal cords:

http://www.starshipsofa.com/blog/2011/10/27/starshipsofa-no-209-mike-allen/*http://www.starshipsofa.com/blog/2009/04/02/aural-delights-no-74-nebula-nominee-mike-allen/

Hal's books are available from bookstores of your choice. His poetry collection *Songs for the Devil and Death* (containing "From the Fragments of Heraklitos") was reviewed in FU#3 and is available from www.papaveria.com. And yes, he also has an online home with loads of Cool Stuff, here: http://www.halduncan.com/.

PAPAVERIA PRESS

WWW.PAPAVERIA.COM

Specialising in limited, handbound editions and the occasional trade paperback, Papaveria is an independent micro-press publishing poetry and prose in the fields of fairy tales, fantasies and myth.

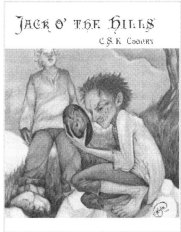

Books are small gods.

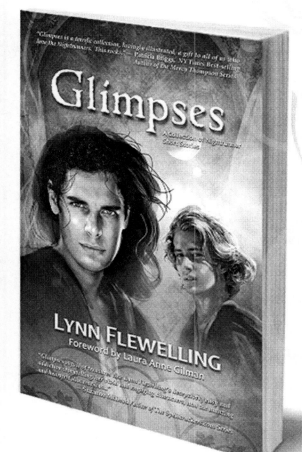

Life Decisions
by
Kaolin Fire

The soul gazes down, through clouds
no living thing can break,
at its character sheet writ large:
"So you're saying I can start
a level seven?" Not too eager—
awed, and humble. Raphael
assures the soul; Michael warns
of worth-inflation: "It will seem
a level five, at best." Monstrous angel wings
shrug.

The soul scribbles fire
across the page of the world, mumbling
"carry one, take off five, that leaves...."
and winces. No, it'll spend more on health,
though something has to be sacrificed
for love. Money? Hardship? Only God
knows the right balance—unless this game
is His knowledge, past and future...

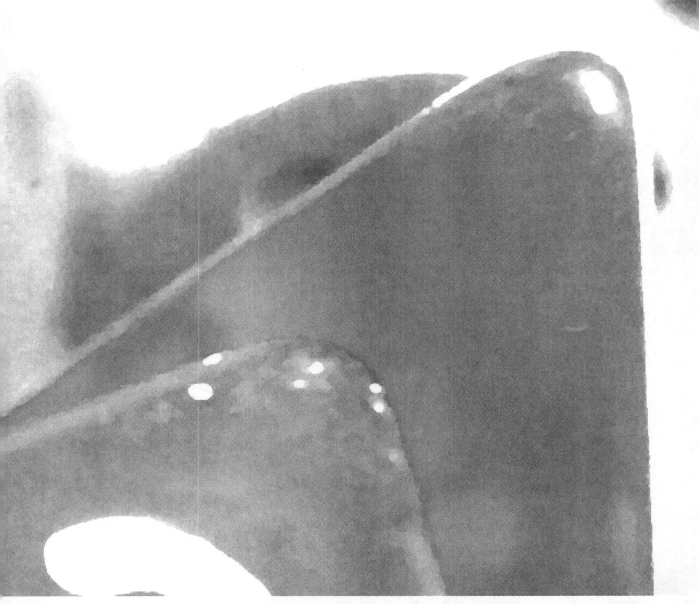

the rule books are incredibly fuzzy
on that subject. Perhaps this time,
the soul thinks, it should be a mystic.

It looks pleadingly up at the two angels:
"Can't he just roll the dice?"

The Bachorum Principle

by
Brenda Stokes Barron

Herein, by the dawn's early light...

In the twenty-second century, a man called Bachorum founded a new settlement on a distant planet. He called the civilization Numerica in honor of what had transpired and what was to come. He stripped the land of features and erected a fortress made of obsidian harvested from Earth just prior to the Abandoning for this very purpose. He had seen the Invaders coming and planned for them.

The masses held him up as their leader because he was Good and he was Pure and he was all Things to all People.

Numerica was much like Earth civilizations with jobs and religions and meeting places until one day Bachorum sat at the top of his fortress overlooking the barren land and wrote the five tenants of the world as he saw it. No more would people gather in the meeting places or earn wages or worship false gods. It was the Bachorum Principle and it contained infinite wisdom. The people bowed down and

92

grovelled in the red dirt, begging to kiss its toes.

—

I was born, as we are all born, of man in his glory. I burst through his stomach and in my life, brought his death. They come in the night and touch my legs for want of forgetting. I feel their breath on my belly, their fingers, so many inside me. They probe, investigate, and watch as I moan and writhe over and over again in awe and mystery and shame. They lie on top of me and grunt and I turn my face to the side, hoping they forget faster. And they do. They forget so much, they remember and spit on me as they leave me raw and broken in the black tent at the bottom of the tower.

I snap my legs together like the sea beast's jaws when they are done. My only rebellion. They will be back tomorrow because they'll remember their need to forget.

—

Tenant #1: Numerica shall be a land of remembering and forgetting.

—

The men pray to God Bachorum and bring bleeding fingertips to parched mouths. They sit at the base of the obsidian tower after leaving our tents and drag their nails in the dirt of

Numerica trying to leave an impression or rid themselves of our scent. I watch them from my tent and giggle. Their very desire for Him to know them is blasphemy in a world where the Pure are the Same.

Their efforts are futile but I cannot speak such insolent things. I laugh on my back into the night. It is only so long before I will have fulfilled my purpose and become Pure at the hands of god's servants.

—

Tenant #2: Do not worship Numerica. Pray to the infinite wisdom of Bachorum for guidance. But do not seek to know Him, for He is unknowable.

—

They say I am flawed and cannot be fixed. They say there is no length of time long enough to make me Pure. Counting is outlawed in Numerica because it indicates a dependence on the past and we don't depend on the past. God Bachorum says the past breeds uncertainty and weakness into our bones and we are not allowed to be weak and unsure unless we seek punishment or death.

I do not want to die. The men with their million hands can count in years for purifying as I can count their hands and fingers for forgetting. It is a sin, to count their purifying hands and blasphemous lips, but I do it anyway. I catalogue their sour kisses in my mind like our ancestors recorded dates of birth in moleskin journals and hand-me-down Bibles.

Tenant #1: Numerica shall be a land of remembering and forgetting.

—

Tenant #3: Numbers are bastions of truth and ignorance. All, every, none, never, nothing are perfect in their precision. Some, both, a few, many, a little, a bit, a tad are weak and of our ancestors. You are Every or you are None. Never both or some.

—

The Timekeepers remind us to pray. I crawl to my knees, exposing the bones of my back and hiding my breasts. The position of the sacred hides my flaws. I am thankful to be Pure for even this moment of prayer to the God who has forsaken me.

When the clocks go quiet, I am on my back again, ready for the forgetters and rememberers.

They have taken the life from my belly. One of many. It was another, like

93

me. Different and impure and wrong, deserving the fate of the tents.

They whisper a future filled with lies in my ear right before they climax. "You will be Pure soon," they say.

I never look them in the eye. I don't want to remember them.

—

Tenant #4: The tower is sacred and to be worshipped. It is the only object in Numerica worth worshipping. When the Timekeepers' clocks strike, all must face the tower and bow and thank it for its many blessings.

—

I am not allowed books in my black tent at the base of the tower but I hear the murmurings of the Pure. They echo out from the obsidian walls and in Bachorum's wails when he decries all that is Not Man. I hear what they say and what they don't say. They remember the Abandoning and what it felt like to be ripped from the world because we were weak. Because we had connections and boundaries and reasons. We loved and shared and compromised. They remember forgetting who they were and finding Numerica a harsh desert for the broken. And more than anything else, they remember forgetting the Other Man. The one of which we are not to speak. The Other Man that wasn't a man at all.

94

They remember us.

I was not born from a man's stomach, even though He says as much. I was born as we are all born and are taught to forget. I gave birth to life new again. This time, an impure one with golden curls. But that is all that I am good for, and even that is not good enough to be remembered. I will be Purified once their forgetting proves futile.

It is easier without us, He says. We are a liability because of our vulnerability. I struggle to hold my breath when the urge comes to speak the impossible words: The Invaders were nothing more than a man's dream. So he became He. And the Invaders became the Impure. And Earth became Numerica. And we are no more vulnerable than He.

—

Tenant #5: Of the Abandoning, one lesson can be learned: do not honor Numerica as you did Earth. Numerica claims only offerings of the weak and impure. The weak are those without obsidian.

—

I do not have obsidian in my blood. I do not have the Purity between my legs.

We lay in the black tents at the base of the obsidian tower waiting to be forgotten. We count men's fingers and toes and know we will not be Purified. We are the offering to Numerica. The sea beast will eat us whole once we've brought enough secret life into this desert world.

We wait for the day when the man named Bachorum has had his fill of Purification. His fill of a desire to right what wronged humanity as he saw it. The Abandoning is only a dream. Maybe one day, someday, on a whim, if He fancies, the tents will be torn down. But we lay and pray and kiss our fingers and rub our bellies hoping the tower will fall.

We wait for Some or Both.

We wait for uncertainty.

We wait for the Other Man whose name we cannot speak (Mother) and we turn our faces from the men in the dark, inching fingers beneath tent flaps to root life back into the cracked soil.

I can see my sister's hand outside of her tent, fingers poised and upright on the ground. And her sister's and her sister's. We count them, one by one, and Bachorum turns a blind eye. He doesn't notice how our hands almost touch. That we've been pushing the tents closer and closer together.

We are many in our tiny blasphemies.

We are an army on its back waiting to be raised.

———————————

Black Sheep
by
Jacqueline West

The morning moon lids its cold eye.
The sky is the hue of a puddle,
liquid tin rippling violet at the rim.

Between the rocks, two ewes
have dropped their lambs. Wet patches
of grass bed their slick heads.

He comes ready to strip the bags
of afterbirth that case spindly limbs,
strange mushrooms of quiet drowning,

but when he nears, he sees
that both are black. Not the black
of wet wool, of morning blood in dim light,

but the black of the devil's fingerprint
smudged down in the sweet grass
of pasture, sinkholes to break the legs

of his innocent flock. It is a mark,
he knows, his own; painted on his head
like a butcher's sign. There is no time.

The knife is sharp against his thigh;
the cuts quick and quiet.
The lambs curl, small and dark,

two seeds that will never
branch out into the doom
hidden deep in their stopped hearts.

THIS INSCRUTABLE LIGHT:
A RESPONSE TO THOMAS LIGOTTI'S THE CONSPIRACY AGAINST THE HUMAN RACE

"IF THERE WERE NO ETERNAL CONSCIOUSNESS IN A MAN, IF AT THE BOTTOM OF EVERYTHING THERE WERE ONLY A WILD FERMENT, A POWER THAT TWISTING IN DARK PASSIONS PRODUCED EVERYTHING GREAT OR INCONSEQUENTIAL; IF AN UNFATHOMABLE, INSATIABLE EMPTINESS LAY HID BENEATH EVERYTHING, WHAT WOULD LIFE BE BUT DESPAIR?"

–SOREN KIERKEGAARD,
FEAR & TREMBLING

EDITORIAL BY BRANDON H. BELL

2010 Bram Stoker Award Nominee

THE
CONSPIRACY
AGAINST THE HUMAN
RACE

THOMAS LIGOTTI

A Nobody's Recollection on Supernatural Horror

I first encountered Ligotti in Douglas Winter's anthology, *Prime Evil*. The story, *Alice's Last Adventure* to my mid-teenage assessment, was Okay. I enjoyed *Orange is for Anguish, Blue for Insanity* and *The Juniper Tree* better. Nonetheless, by the time I read *Nethescurial* in Weird Tales, I'd come across the news that Ligotti was the next big thing in Horror (soon after that, Robert McCammon jumped ship along with a bunch of folks playing Nietzsche to the genre.)

I picked up *Songs of a Dead Dreamer* and understood the hubbub. Even as horror was pronounced dead, here arrived a writer working very much in the weird tradition of Poe and Lovecraft, who yet refrained (most of the time) from bogging down in a morass of words or simply regurgitating tales of the type of monsters that now bear the label Love-craftian. Ligotti wrote fictional lectures on Horror as horror stories. He wrote from a conceptual space, informed by a jaundiced perception of the universe. Not satisfied with parroting a milieu or method, Ligotti posited a cosmos not merely indifferent and filled with things

vast and harmful, but one pernicious in its malignancy. His was a world filled with bad, be it sentient, instinctual, or the simple state of things, that tended to both awareness of and animosity toward humankind.

This is better, my younger self concluded.

By the time I finished *Grimscribe*, I came to a realization about Ligotti's work: though often brilliant, sometimes florid, it existed in THAT universe. The tone didn't vary. It addled the brain when consumed like I would writer's work back then: reading everything they'd written to the exclusion of all else. The effect could be intoxicating.

I'm not interested in carrying the topic of Ligotti's fiction much further. It's good stuff, and if you haven't read it you should. Instead it is his recent non-fiction book, *The Conspiracy Against the Human Race*, that has me excited. I'd like to do something more audacious than I have any right to do, and offer an answer to Ligotti.

I recommend reading *The Conspiracy Against the Human Race* (TCATHR). The reader should be warned about this real-life *King In Yellow*: a work of such unremitting bleakness that will lay ruin to all that you hold dear... If you are not prepared to answer Ligotti.

When I first heard about TCATHR I thought, based on my previous reading, that I knew the sort of claims he'd make. I also suspected that mine was an uncommon philosophical position from which to call Ligotti. Call as in, I'll meet your fiver and raise you 'all in.' It is all in, too, because Ligotti's charge is a simple one.

What worth is life?

Mr. Ligotti's answer is: nothing. In fact, life is not worth living.

Once I read the book, I took a deep breath and considered his positions. I noted a lack of actual responses to the charges Ligotti makes of existence. In looking through the reviews of the book, all that I found fell into three basic positions:

1. Ligotti's got it right! I 'get it' too!
2. Ug, I read this? and
3. Waste of time except as a key for understanding his work.

No one I've noted has offered a considered answer to Ligott's claims. I'd like to do that here, and I don't need a whole book to do it. Like his fiction, TCATHR soars into brilliance only to get bogged down in the nihilism it seeks to espouse. Toward the end of the book, in all caps, the author, I guess you might say 'exclaims,' "EVERYTHING IN EXISTENCE IS MALIGNANTLY USELESS!"

Whoa there, kimosabe.

I will summarize Ligotti's claims, then outline different ways we may view existence. Last we'll look at how we'd answer Ligotti from those alternate positions and I'll conclude with what I feel is the most robust answer.

This is perhaps The Question in one's existence. If the reader carries this into conversation elsewhere, I'll consider this a success. In particular, I'd like to offer a rationale for those folks who find themselves unable to latch on to the 'Revealed Truth exists' position I'll describe below, but remain of the mindset that life is worth living.

Oh, and a few notes on my approach. Like Ligotti, I'm no philosopher, and while I'm happy to draw from those sources, I don't claim to use my terms with the rigor expected of a philosopher. Due to the nature of some of Ligotti's claims, I address him on a level I would typically consider off-limits. This is not an attack on the man, but rather an argument based on facts at hand and the position he takes. My belief is that Ligotti is a sentient being who yearns for happiness and wishes not to suffer. I fear one day I will pick up the paper and find he made good on his pronouncement about the value of life. That would be a tragedy. Ligotti speculates that pessimism may be chemically ordained: something one may not overcome. It is also conceivable that pessimism is a coping mechanism like any other belief system, and shouldn't be overcome.

That acknowledged, let's begin.

The Truth Positions

Position One: There is no revealed truth. Whatever the nature of existence, no one is talking, there may not be anyone to talk, and it is up to us to determine a functional definition of truth... or not. That too is up to us.

Position Two: There is a Revealed Truth. All questions are answered and there is no ambiguity, or what little their might be are matters of degrees/denominational choices. One could reject the Revealed Truth but one would be wrong.

Position Three: There is Truth but it is not revealed. There is no way we can be certain to know this Truth. Our conclusions are inferences only. There are reasons we infer this Truth that remains unrevealed.

Position Four: Truth exists but there is no Revelation per se; it is revealed via experience. Some process or set of processes or practices lead to an understanding of truth. Truth, in this understanding, is not a belief, but an experience or the results of the fore-mentioned process/practice.

Ancillary to the Four Positions: I decide the Truth (or lack thereof), and so do you.

102

Ligotti's Assertions

- **Consciousness is an existential liability, and the source of all horror and suffering, due to the awareness of sickness, suffering, and death.**

- **Life, the Universe, and everything is MALIGNANTLY USELESS. All caps on that one, every time.**

- **Through various tactics, we are actors in the biological conspiracy against ourselves, compelling us to believe that life is worth living.**

- **We are not real. Consciousness fools us into believing that we are real instead of a puppet of our biology. We are akin to supernaturally animate puppets, who believe themselves real.**

- **Life is not worth living.**

- **Because existence is composed of suffering (mostly) procreation may rightly be deemed an act of violence against the unborn.**

- **And, all this in mind, the human race should stop procreating, at least, or perhaps engage in a species-wide suicide.**

Some of these points are paraphrased, but present the essence of Ligotti's assertions.

Both Ligotti and the author of the foreword, Ray Brassier, make short order of the most obvious objection to Ligotti, that the mere act of writing is a life-affirming action in contradiction to his stated position. Essentially, Ligotti is mired in the same condition and, thus functioning, cannot be faulted for maneuvering that condition with whatever coping mechanisms at his disposal, especially if they shed light on our predicament.

Fair enough, but this is where the crack in his doctrine begins.

Jesus loves me?

"The modern hero, the modern individual who dares to heed the call and seek the mansion of that presence with whom it is our whole destiny to be atoned, cannot, indeed must not, wait for his community to cast off its slough of pride, fear, rationalized avarice, and sanctified misunderstanding. "Live," Nietzsche says, "as though the day were here." It is not society that is to guide and save the creative hero, but precisely the reverse. And so every one of us shares the supreme ordeal—carries the cross of the redeemer—not in the bright moments of his tribe's great victories, but in the silences of his personal despair." —Joseph Campbell

Ligotti presents the writing of Richard Double, Thomas Metzinger, and other cognitive psychologists, philosophers, and neuroscientists to make the argument that we are acting out "the tragedy of the ego" as mechanistic simulations of personhood.

In an aside of sorts, we are told in TCATHR that no one can really, fully be a determinist and remain sane. It is a constant hedging that grows tiresome.

I don't have the time, space, or expertise to adequately cover the state of the art in cognitive theory. Peter Watts gives a great treatment of these ideas in his first-contact novel, *Blindsight*, and mentions Metzinger's *Being No One* as the toughest book he's ever read. In his *Blindsight* notes, Watts briefly and in lively fashion describes Metzinger's hypothesis about the subjective sense of self and why ego would emerge in cognitive systems like us homosapiens. Watts suggests it would be easier to list those who haven't tried to explain consciousness, and mentions theories from diffuse electrical fields, quantum puppet shows, and a range of conjectured physical locations of consciousness in the brain.

The question to Watts is: What good is consciousness? He provides examples where consciousness is effectively kept out of the decision process because it just isn't as good at it (think of that drive home you can barely remember,

103

and you have an example of this from everyday life.) Aesthetics might be an exception, an area where self-awareness is needed. Interesting, given Ligotti's own sense that aesthetics represent a valid domain. But the cost of sentience? It may ultimately be that of extinction because aesthetics entails the ability to gain unearned rewards. Negative feedback loop.

It is, to my mind, a reductionist take on our situation as sentient beings, but when posed as a question of evolutionary adaptiveness, over Ligotti's "Is life worth living?"/EVERYTHING IS MALIGNANTLY USELESS conceptual dyad, it is a more anchored and useful meditation on the subject. This idea of sentience as evolutionary liability is not new to readers of fantastic fiction (the Shaper-Mechanist stories from Bruce Sterling spring to mind, among others) and I suspect we'll see more populist explorations of these ideas to come.

Ligotti cites valid sources. The function of consciousness is a valid talking point. To be clear: I don't suggest a denial of the truths Metzinger and others like him discover. That consciousness is an emergent system, as opposed to a pit at the center of our individual avocados, is very likely true. Metzinger suggests a naive realism is our nature, but also says that we "can wake up from our biological history."

Whatever our nature as sentient beings, *Cogito ergo sum*. Furthermore, Ligotti never suggests the ultimate hell of being, that of solipsism. And he bases his affront at existence on the endless suffering of sentient beings.

The suffering is real. The sufferers are not.

This is meaningless.

Whatever systems give rise to these sufferers, within that system they are functionally real. We are real. Or, we are no more or less real than anything else. I invoke the law of the excluded middle. One could still say: the suffering is not real, and neither are we. I don't agree, but it would at least be a logical position. It would make meaningless a statement like EVERYTHING IS MALIGNANTLY USELESS. Since we all, including Ligotti, believe in the reality of the suffering, then let us acknowledge this fallacy in the position that we are fake but our suffering is real.

What about warrantability? Most of what we regard as warranted is little more than things that we believe, like 'Jesus loves me' or EVERYTHING IS MALIGNANTLY USELESS. We can believe these things, but they are hard to prove, which relates back to our positions on revealed truth. I find a similar failure when talking about correspondence tests for the truth. The faithful Christian will say "Of course Jesus loves me," and Ligotti will say EVERYTHING IS MALIGNANTLY USELESS. Both speak with equal conviction, and with assurances to their cogency. And both views (and many others besides) would pass a coherence test, even though they are diametrically opposed views and thus they cannot both be true. Warrants, correspondence, and coherence tests don't help us much in this dialog.

When faced with a truth test based on pragmatism, though, the Ligotti position does not fare well. We could cite various pursuits that a reasonable person would deem worthwhile, and even Ligotti would agree that creative works appealing to a sense of aesthetics have validity and worth, and on this basis we can say that living as though today were the day, as Nietzsche said—as though we have work to do and a purpose to fill—carries with it a pragmatism that Ligotti's pessimism lacks.

In Search of...

Any of the Truth positions could take a pessimistic, ambivalent, or optimistic mode. Ligotti's is a pessimistic Position One (no revealed Truth.) For many readers, the conversation ended with the list of his assertions. These ideas are idiotic and wrong at a glance. This stance is particularly bolstered by a Position Two on the Truth question (there is a Revealed Truth.) These folks are often followers of a religious tradition, fundamentalist in their interpretation, though other backgrounds are conceivable. The defining characteristic of this mode is belief that one has access to Truth as revealed by an ultimate Source or Ground of Being. Typically this is God, Allah, Brahma, though nontheists like some of the more strident Nichiren Buddhist and more dualistic eastern traditions could fall under this mode.

These folks have found the Truth. They have the answers to the questions of the universe, provided them via a holy text or texts of divine origin. Perhaps some have living prophets who speak on behalf of the Absolute. Such a position, Ligotti notes, reflects the multifarious nature of Truth despite our tendency to believe Truth a monolithic thing. I don't believe a revealed Truth exists, or at least it has not yet been revealed. But for the person who does, all this talk adds up to so much belly gazing and liberal pessimism.

And yet, Ligotti's book was a finalist for the 2010 Bram Stoker awards, signifying that at least some significant portion of the community aware of nonfiction works related to the horror genre, considered this book among the most important of the year. Ligotti's oeuvre to date suggests his place among writers like Lovecraft, Poe, and Beckett is assured. Ligotti has called us all on our ensnarement in a world of becoming and unbridled desire. Ligotti is, on these points, absolutely correct. If you have a Revealed Truth, then lucky you. You can toss aside this dour read and pursue some other pastime.

Position Three on Truth says there is a Truth, but it has not been revealed. Functionally no different than Position One, but for one odd quirk a human being is capable. Faith. This is the faith of the Gnostic perhaps, the liberal Christian, Jew, or Muslim. It is the faith of the theist who claims no specific religious ties. This person of faith acknowledges the human origin of the given holy book (thus no revelation) but uses it nonetheless as a guide for living. She has faith, while knowing there is no way to know or to prove the object of worship is real or True. Some might say that it is the act of faith that matters.

This is, in my estimation, the most defensible western religious mode, when applied to one's self and one's life. When coupled with an evangelical zeal, it morphs into the most grating. Those folks think they've found the Truth, and think you should find the same. Because there really is no revealed Truth (unlike Ligotti, I will cry foul on the idea of unending relativism [which I understand is contradictory on the surface as I declare 'there is no Revealed Truth,' but bear with me...]) all traditional religious people fall into the type three position. Some of them just don't know it.

Finally Position Four suggests there is

106

a Truth, but it is revealed through experience. Here is the Buddhist path, where belief is only ever a raft to cross a river or stream, but not the destination. Truth is ephemeral, subjective, and given more to heuristics than commandments. Truth is not easy. But along that path lies the solution to suffering and its causes.

Carl Sagan's might be a good example of an optimist Position One. No revealed Truth, and yet his perception of the universe, its beauty, served him.

Ligotti says of Truth:

"Renowned for stating his convictions in the form of a paradox, as above, Chesterton, along with anyone who has something positive to say about the human race, comes out on top in the crusade for truth. (There is nothing paradoxical about that.) Therefore, should your truth run counter to that of individuals who devise or applaud paradoxes that stiff up the status quo, you would be well advised to take your arguments, tear them up, and throw them in someone else's garbage."

Ligotti here refers to the tendency of human optimists, in this case a Christian apologist, to treat logic as secondary, irrelevant, or as a liability, and once Truth is reached via paradox, metaphor, faith, intuition, or a myriad other contrivances, the conversation is at a close. Through inference, Ligotti may also suggest that logic followed without sentimentalism or irrational thought-structures would lead one to a pessimistic conclusion. Ligotti, while claiming a Pessimistic Position One (no Revealed Truth) in fact exposes himself as a Position Four seeker (Truth exists but is not Revealed except through experience) who has lapsed in the face of Revelation into a Position Two believer (Revealed Truth exists.)

I think he said 'yo mama.'

"The unconscious is always the fly in the ointment, the skeleton on the cupboard of perfection, the painful lie given all idealistic pronouncements, the earthliness that clings to our human nature and sadly clouds the crystal clarity we long for. In the alchemical view, rust, like verdigris, is the metal's sickness. But at the same time this leprosy is the vera prima materia, the basis for the preparation of the philosophical gold." —**Carl Jung, Dreams**

We divided up our positions in our conversation with Ligotti based on the question: "Is there a Revealed Truth?" It would have been obvious to readers of TCATHR to instead ask, "Is life worth living?" and to general seekers after Truth (at least in the West), "Does God exist?" and perhaps secondarily, "Does He [sic] love us?"

Critically examined, our four categories have a problem, don't they?

There is no Revealed Truth. Fair enough.

There is a Revealed Truth. Also fair.

There is a Truth but it is not Revealed. Ligotti won't be the only one to roll his eyes. Basically here stands Chesterton and his derision of logic. Here is the faith that Christians speak of (the honest ones, at least.) We are prevaricating, our language lacks precision, our thoughts are not cogent. I suggest the stance is different enough from the certainties of the first two positions to warrant consideration. Even though so many who advocate for the position, as they become 'stronger in their faith' grow to believe that along with their faith, hope, and charity, they also received the Bat Phone.

Last there is Truth, but it is not Revealed and found only through practice. The objection is: if the Truth exists, at some point it is found. And thus we have our Revealed Truth and no need for a separate category. I suggest a different understanding of what Truth means gives rise to validity. This understanding of truth is purely experiential. The path may be defined but not the experience. The map written, but the journey must be undertaken by each who would have understanding. And that understanding is only ever provisional, incomplete, and never quite the encompassing Truth with a capital T that the first two positions deny or proclaim.

Ligotti never comes right out an states as much, but from his criticism of Chesterton's flippancy toward logic, it is fair to infer that Ligotti views himself as a champion of logic in the question of 'Is life worth living?' Using logical deduction, studying the work of others who seem to see what he also perceives, and applying the true-state experience of the depressed mind, Ligotti has followed a path leading to Revelation. Ligotti holds the Truth of the entire universe. He has dropped anchor, as all believers are wont, and after some consideration as to its merits, chosen to share with the world the Truth that he has found.

Now read that last paragraph over again with this understanding: not sarcastic in tone and written by a man that is no believer in any theological dogma; who is, in fact, an atheist.

I no more agree with Chesterton than I do with Ligotti but I will give Chesterton this much more credit over Ligotti: though he may be the sort that evangelises a doctrine he surmises to be True (something I have nothing but contempt for) on the face of it he at least realizes that logic cannot justify his position. Ligotti contrariwise would have us believe that he exposes the meat grinder Truth. There is no path ahead, there is no uncertainty, and there is no room for dis-

agreement with this John the Baptist of Pessimism. One cannot argue or disagree with Ligotti's position without essentially proving his premise, that we are unwitting automata working against our own best interest—aka our annihilation.

Because, recall, Ligotti believes himself to be a wooden puppet, come to life: a 'not real' thing, realizing itself in the stage of horror that is consciousness. As a Buddhist, I don't believe in an immortal soul. According to the doctrine of Dependant Origination, which in its most basic form states 'because of this, that', we are aggregate things, us sentient beings. From all the non-human components the universe brings to bear, humans are formed, consciousness included. Buddhism allows for a clear understanding of the suffering and its causes that Ligotti perceives and uses as the basis for his doctrine of hopelessness. But Ligotti, like many Christian critics of Buddhism (strange bedfellows, indeed!), stops short of a full and honest account of the picture this philosophy of the mind (that sometimes plays at being a religion) offers.

I don't want to 'go all Buddhist on ya' and in particular I intend this to remain foremost a humanist document. Nonetheless, Ligotti singles out Buddhism, and in this point only will I follow suit. Buddhism is based on suffering and its causes, but does not stop there. The last two of the Four Noble Truths are: The cessation of suffering and the causes of that cessation. In other words, this doctrine does not try to paint a happy face on the disatisfatoriness of the world, but offers a prognosis and a prescription that suggests while life may have no cure, there is a treatment.

With that I'll return to my humanist-orientation by offering a counter to his living puppet analogy. Instead of the stark uncanny-valley puppet-on-its-strings, lurching about an empty stage, screaming a silent scream, one presumes, I suggest human beings—perhaps any sentience that arises in the universe—are more akin to that other genre trope of emergent intelligence: the AI, born; the life that arises out of software and wires and a billions connections. Such an intelligence might pursue any sort of existence it chooses; it might find the universe a place of wonder or horror. It could posit for itself any role.

And, thus, humanity.

Can you see the real me?

"'One must go further, one must go further.' This need to go on is of ancient standing. Heraclitus the 'obscure' who reposited his thoughts in his writings in the Temple of Diana (for his thoughts had been his armour in life, which he therefore hung up in the temple of the goddess), the obscure Heraclitus had said 'one can never walk through the same river twice.' The obscure Heraclitus had a disciple who didn't remain standing there but went further and added, 'One cannot do it even once.' Poor Heraclitus to have such a disciple! This improvement changed the Heraclitian principle into an Eleatic doctrine denying movement, and yet all that disciple wanted was to be a disciple of Heraclitus who went further, not back to what Heraclitus had abandoned." —Soren Kierkegaard, Fear and Trembling

One must ask of Ligotti, "what does real mean?"

How is it that these imaginary or fake things that we are experience real suffering? Would we be real if there was some pith at our center that did not end? Is it this lack of god-stuff that makes us irreal? Ligotti mourns for a Ground of Being that is not there. A Shore that might stand strong against the tides of time, and in a deficit of such, he cries out in an empty universe, this wooden puppet that has realized itself for what it is, in anger, grief, horror.

If we start from the assumption that there is no god-stuff, nothing more or less eternal than anything else, our perspective shifts. My pain is an affliction of my own attachment to that which I never could hold or own. Why did I ever believe otherwise? Maybe I needed that belief, because I am a small and frail

109

thing and there is so much I do not understand.

"In a universe suddenly divested of illusions and lights, man feels an alien, a stranger. His exile is without remedy since he is deprived of the memory of a lost home or the hope of a promised land. This divorce between man and his life, the actor and his setting, is properly the feeling of absurdity." —**Albert Camus, An Absurd Reasoning: Absurdity and Suicide**

And there, lost, alone, hopeless, we may remain. Or we could proclaim some revelation of Truth, and hope to convince ourselves of its veracity. Or we could take the next step into an emptiness neither nihilistic nor revelatory. The emptiness of our own nature.

"What did I learn from my teacher? Nothing! He took everything away from me. When I became attached to what he was saying, he took it away from me. By meeting him I had taken everything away from me..... He crushed and crushed and completely crushed me.... He never let one hang on to anything. And that was his theory of teaching Buddhism.... After he died, people called me a heretic, but I am not good enough to have a heresy, because I have nothing. There is no Pure Land or Zen or Buddhism or philosophy. Nothing to hang on to. Nothing controls me. I was raised as a real, free man. And I am deeply grateful...." —**Haya**

110

Akegarasu, Shout of Buddha

Go Further

It would be easy, to get stuck with Ligotti, his book like some modern day surrogate to Heraclitus' disciple.

The fault of Ligotti's argument is the fault of every argument that posits to depict the end of all questions, to portray the Truth, of a whole and defined cloth. Because it requires one to stop questioning and accept. And though Ligotti will deny such an interpretation, he has, just like those religious folks who believe you are going to hell if you don't join them, come up with a bulletproof rationale for why we might object and by doing so prove our participation in his conspiracy. It's all a little too neat.

In the final analysis, I find myself, despite myself, giving a favorable review to the position of Faith, and have quoted Keirkegaard not once but twice in this treatment. As soon as Faith (aka Truth exists but is not Revealed) morphs into doctrinal or dogmatic certainty (aka Revealed Truth exists), as is the case with most modern religious movements, it becomes a liability to the seeker.

Ascendant over all the positions on the revealed truth question is Position Four: Truth exists but is revealed only through experience, with the caveat being the experiential and subjective nature of that truth. When, as with Ligotti, our search leads us to a Revealed Truth that kills inquiry and offers some final summation of existence, the Truth exposes itself as tarnished, rusted, a forgery.

What Ligotti offers us is a deep look into suffering and its reality. Don't stop, as Ligotti advocates. Mine is not a suggestion for Buddhism or any particular path, other than endless inquiry and curiosity. Although I did want to note that Science fits the bill as a valid position four (Truth exists but may be revealed only via experience.) How cool is that?

These ideas and considerations are not in the realm of philosophers, scientists, writers, poets, monks, priests, and outside of the realm of the every day person. In the end, only each individual may decide what the ultimate Truth of the universe might be. I choose to believe in a path forward that is rational, and in which I might never cease to find wonder in the present moment, and to find strength to stand against the suffering that will come, and to remember that once I gave you, Dear Reader, a wink and said...

Who ya gonna trust? Me, or the weird wooden dummy beside me?

At the Crossroads of the West
by
J. C. Runolfson

a wager, Loki says
and Coyote never could resist.
They drink fermented honey
distilled cactus to seal the deal.
Gold on red on gold
sun-stealers, bloodslayers, shapechangers
tricksters.
Loki smiles sly
slips into the fever dreams of a wayward prophet
whispers, this is the place.
What other god would do such a thing?
Bring the white plague, bring the soldiers,
the pioneers settling Coyote's land,
harrying and harassing and killing his prey, his family.
Coyote retaliates, drought and the locusts,
the lake of salt, the high desert
forge of god, but
which god would use such an anvil?
Such hammer and tongs, such fire
and then the plunge into quenching cold.
Loki knows ice and snow
but this white powder fury is a different thing
for which he calls on Jack.
Jack-in-the-Green, Jack-a-nape, Jackdaw,
come be Jack Frost for me, he says,
we got a point to prove.
Jack won't rouse for less than the water of life
usquebaugh, barley beer, blood.
Among these teetotalers, he takes the last
red on white on red
stone and sand under the snow under the blood
under the red skin and the white.
Coyote sees the carrion and knows
this invader hedges his bets.

112

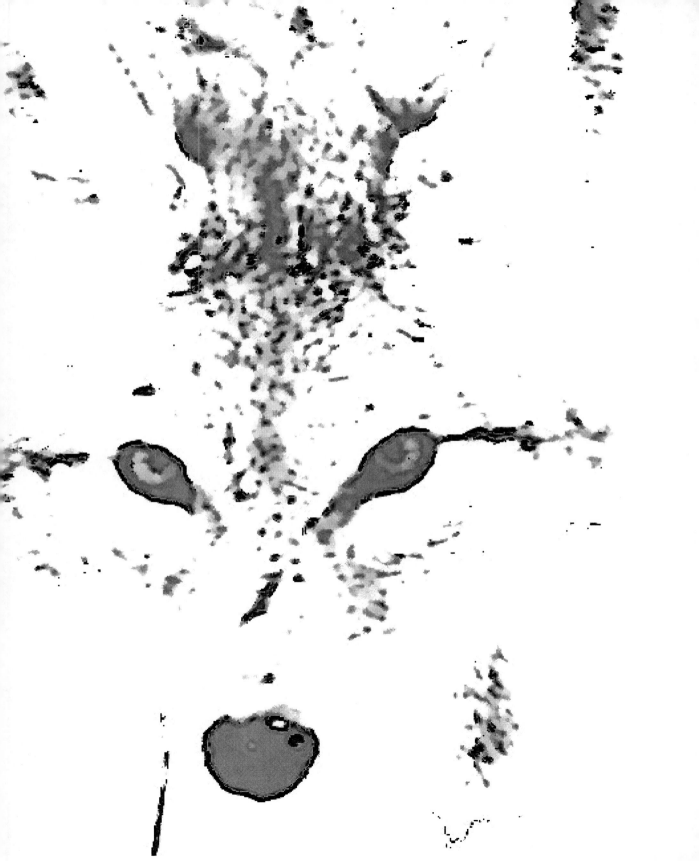

Stolen Souls

by
Mike Allen

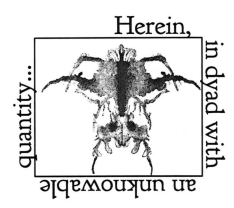

Herein, *in dyad with* an unknowable ...quantity...

1. Incident in Downtown Pittsburgh

The ghorlem jabbed the business end of its TachyBlaz in Venner's face, nearly ramming both barrels up the human's nose. Driving Venner backward until he was pressed against the aluminum alley wall, it spat out in rapid-fire Anglo: "Out with them." *Owtwitum*, it sounded like. "You know what I want." *Uno watiwand*. With each utterance green-brown vapor wafted from the back of its adze-shaped head. The exoveins that stretched from its chin to its shoulders pulsed with anticipation. "Take them out, now. Give them to me!"

Venner curled his upper lip into a sneer, and snarled a defiant Anglo curse. His assailant seized him by the throat with one twenty-fingered hand. Four fingers of the other tightened on TachyBlaz triggers. "Will cut your arms and legs off. Then take them out while you still scream."

With a cry he grabbed for the ghor-

116

lem's eyestalks. It flexed its trigger fingers. Twin pinpricks of light flashed out from the TachyBlaz, slicing through Venner's unisuit, slashing white-hot across his chest.

Venner screamed. "No! Wait!"

"No time to wait," the ghorlem frothed. It constricted its grip around Venner's neck, and adjusted its aim to sever his right arm at the shoulder.

Venner grimaced in terror. "I'll find someone else for you. Someone worth a thousand times more. Please!"

"No. You are what I want. Give it up nice, I'll spare you pain."

He choked back a sob. When the ghorlem let go of his throat, he sank to the asphalt, weeping in denial, until the alien jabbed its TachyBlaz against the top of his skull. Then Venner stroked a patch behind his left ear with a trembling hand, letting the scanner there register his fingertip pattern and pulse.

He closed his eyes with a gasp, and shut down. Became immobile. Died. The top of his head folded open in quarter sections.

Unbeknownst to the ghorlem, motosensors implanted in the rims of Venner's ears continued to watch.

Venner's assailant stared greedily into the naked skull-casing. The cortex revealed inside was a highly-experimental model, sure to bring a hefty bonus from the ringbosses off-world. The ghorlem chortled—a noise like the gagging of a drowning human—and reached into Venner's head to pluck out the goods.

The cortex throbbed strangely inside the cage of the ghorlem's spindly fingers, but when it plopped its prize into the presercase slung underneath its cape, the strange pulsations ceased.

Once it made sure the presercase was securely sealed, the ghorlem made off with its booty.

The 'sensors in Venner's ears tracked the ghorlem until it scurried out of range. Rerouted nerves relayed the information to the brain-case housed in Venner's ample belly, where his real cortex was hidden, safe from thieves.

Once enough time had passed, he returned his respiratory and circulatory systems to their full speed. His head resealed. He opened his eyes and stood up, dusting off his olive-drab unisuit. The twin lacerations from the TachyBlaz still smarted, but a quick inspection proved they weren't serious.

He peered down the alley after his adversary, now long gone. His gaze wandered out the alley-mouth, across the shimmering expanse of the hover-drone landing-strip, into downtown Pittsburgh. Great cylindrical factories perched atop impossibly slender scaffolding, roped together with sinewy fiberoptic cables. Pneumatron lifts crawled along the girders like mechanical slugs. Hoverdrones caution-striped like titanic bumblebees swarmed overhead, their gigagram loads of alloy slung pendulously beneath them. Pittsburgh rose from the continent like a vast insect mound, layer after layer of podment clusters and factories and monorail tubes piled haphazardly toward the stratosphere. Here, among its highest levels, the Downtown industrial complex stretched away from Venner like a shimmering metal web supporting hundreds of titanic egg-cases.

Even now the cortex-thief would be clambering down the scaffolding beneath the landing-strip, the presercase slung behind its back, hoping to lose itself in the crowded dwelling zones below. Venner settled on the edge of an

In the plush pink lobby of the Coital Center, when he and Alys had agreed to become cohabitants, Venner readily confessed his reason for the choice: she reminded him so much of his 'pod-mom.

empty disposal vat. There was nothing he could do but wait. For now, he was helpless.

His lips curled into a snarl as he remembered the day he'd come home to find Alys lying in the middle of the living room, her head wrenched to one side, her hazel eyes bulging in shock. She'd put up such a fight, her attackers couldn't force her to deactivate, so they'd pinned her down and cut into her skull while she was still fully conscious.

She'd been stolen. Venner couldn't even guess what manner of thing she'd been sliced up and recombined with. The cortex that housed her mind had been a neurological gem. . . .

In the plush pink lobby of the Coital Center, when he and Alys had agreed to become cohabitants, Venner readily confessed his reason for the choice: she reminded him so much of his 'pod-mom. He'd tried to explain his 'pod-mom to her—how she'd let him suckle. From the moment they'd installed the cortex in his incubator-grown body, his 'pod-mom treated him like one of the 'womb-grown' from a thousand years gone. She didn't 'wean like a guillotine' as the older kids called it, just suddenly cut him off. She'd eased him out of the physical dependency of infancy, saving him a lot of complexes. She'd handled her job

118

with great mindframe.

When he was done stammering, he was certain he'd blown it; but Alys smiled at him with those gloriously gap-ridden teeth and thanked him for the compliment.

Alys didn't look at all like his 'pod-mom: more muscle than fat, more sinew than soft, a solid, broad chest in place of his 'mom's generous mammaries. She could certainly hold up her end of a piece of heavy furniture. Whenever she came home from her post at the smelting plant, he'd greet her with steaming hot chocolate, and she'd smiled at him with those wondrously crooked teeth. She'd had a great mindframe, better even than his 'pod-mom's.

Stolen. Sliced apart. Bargained away to become a component for some hyperspace privateer's navigation system, to be the lobotomized motor from some automaton slave's body. . . .

The possibilities were endless.

He'd tried to replace her. The mind in the new cortex was named Ophelia. A biofuel contamination had rendered her old body inoperable. Venner picked her because she seemed so much like Alys in the personality profile, but from the moment she'd first peered out of those hazel eyes, she hated him. She told Venner he was a sick mother-fixated freak, and had surgery to re-align those teeth he'd so adored.

Not a trace of his Alys could be

found. The search launched through CorVice combed fifteen planets and dozens of stations, used up all his credit, and turned up nothing.

She'd been stolen, and he could do nothing about it.

The sound of shuffling feet, slow and zombie-like, roused him from his reverie. The ghorlem who assaulted him had returned. Its dark silhouette appeared in the alley mouth, the outline of its head strangely distorted—a cancerous lump rode atop its crown. The alien meandered toward Venner in a daze, its eyestalks drooping, its exoveins lax, green vapors rising in a choked-off trickle from the back of its newly-malformed head.

Venner smiled. The sting worked.

He slid off the disposal vat, and went to greet his captive. Knowing the hapless ghorlem could still hear, he spoke. "I can just imagine what is was like for you." He seized a knobby shoulder and spun the alien around. "Trying to find your next foothold when the 'case on your back starts to twitch, twisting your eyes to look but it's underneath your cape, all you see is something moving under there, and it's cutting its way out of the 'case." A mass of grey matter had clamped spidery metal legs into the ridged flesh on the back of the ghorlem's head: a mobile mind-sapper.

Venner steadied the alien, then gently took hold of the mind-sapper with both hands. "Then you feel those sharp little legs start digging into your skin, you squeal and squeal, and it's crawling up your body. You try to shake it off, but you can't, because you'll lose your grip, and then you'll fall, and fall, and fall."

The pulsing mass scanned and recognized his touch, coiled its legs back into their hidden pouches, slowly withdrew all the monofilaments of neurofiber it had used to pierce the ghorlem's skull cavity.

"And those legs dig in just above your neck, you thrash your head, but it grips so tight, and it hurts so much, and then you feel a hundred neurofibers burrow into your skull. It's a mind-sapper, and it's going to find out everything you know. You get to feel all those tiny 'fibers pierce your brain cavity, and then it completely takes you over. . . "

As the mind-sapper withdrew its last 'fiber, the ghorlem collapsed in an unconscious heap. Now Venner had to wait again, while the device pulsing in his hands autosterilized itself. He tried to clear his mind, to wipe the rictus of rage from his face.

But he couldn't help thinking: if Alys could have had one of these secret abdominal brain-cases that CorVice officers used to hide their real cortex

119

from Brainthieves. . . if Alys had one of these when she was attacked, she'd be coming home from the smelting plant this afternoon to a cup of his hot chocolate.

He'd protested to his superiors at Cor-Vice: "You've got to make them available. People can't protect themselves!" But his superiors insisted knowledge of the second braincase had to be kept confidential, or the Brainthieves would know to look for them. When Venner continued his protests, he was ordered to either desist or report to the surgeons to have his implants removed.

The muscles at the corners of Venner's jaw bulged; he ground his teeth, and thought grimly, *Just one-a-the great dilemmas of Modern Life.*

The 'sapper chimed. It was ready to be reinstalled. As Venner placed the device back inside his head, he reminded himself: it *isn't just Alys you're looking for. If you find anything, a way to trace any of the victims, you've done some good.* He wanted to believe a thread of altruism governed his actions, that he didn't join CorVice just to continue his hopeless search. Even with eighteen successful stings under his belt, he'd found no trace of Alys.

With the mind-sapper reconnected to his neural net, Venner prepared to make his preliminary survey of the replicated memories, to spend a seconds-long lifetime peering out through the stalked

120

eyes of an alien.

It was time to find out what this ghorlem knew.

2. Incident on Tau Ceti Station, One Terran Year Later

Venner stood in absolute darkness, with long, strong fingers clamped like vices around his neck, elbows, and wrists. The motosensors in his ears detected over a dozen humans and ghorlems clustered around him in the warehouse. His captors held him fast, waiting in silence for the Ritual of Disapproval to begin.

A lone spotlight sliced through the black, illuminating a small round dais. Three aliens squatted around the dais, two ghorlems and a vorboros, all with heads bowed. The harsh glare brightened the ghorlems' dun skin membranes to a glistening tan, while it pierced right through the vorboros, refracting a thousand ways inside its crystalline contractile tissue, throwing opaque internal organs into dark relief.

Venner knew their names, although he'd never seen any of the trio in person before. The large pale ghorlem with the wide head was called Grendel by his underlings. The smaller one with the blotchy pigmentation and its empathically-linked vorboros symbiote were known rather picaresquely as Gog and

Magog, though Venner wasn't sure which was which.

The dais phased to a Terran-sky color, and a figure materialized upon it, a short frail human male standing rigid and terrified, eyes flicking desperately back and forth. Venner realized with a chill he was watching a holo, a slo-mo recording of the final moments of the last person who endured the Ritual.

With a soundless scream, the man stepped back, his arms rising to protect his face, and then slugs were bursting him open, TachyBlaz beams were cutting him apart. In seconds he'd been reduced to lifeless pulp and shattered implant components.

Grendel and Gog and Magog made no motion at all, even when the holo faded from their midst.

A rapid-fire gurgle in Venner's ear, a ghorlem's voice: "They want you come." The hands restraining him released their collective grip. Venner obeyed.

Under the spotlight's glare, he prayed the extent of his external alterations wouldn't become too apparent. His jaw once sharp and square, now softened by adipose injections, adjusted back to create an overbite. Nostrils, eyelids, ears re-cut to slant at different angles. His teeth removed, replaced with a new set slightly too big for his oral phenotype. Only his belly remained basically the same, just a little more ample than it was a year ago, when he made the sting

in Downtown Pittsburgh.

His abdominal braincase, too, had been extensively modified. A huge risk, that, because exposing it marked him as CorVice—but he'd scattered his credit around, not gone to the same golem-tech lab in the same star system twice, relying on the vast webs of protective misinformation generated in the Underbelly nets to cover his tracks. The Brainthieves in this chamber knew him as 'Turncoat', someone who sold CorVice secrets to anyone who'd pay; but his real name and the motives that drove him remained safely buried.

A small red circle appeared in the center of the dais. The Ritual of Disapproval had begun.

Venner kept his face smooth as glass. *You wanted this*, he told himself, and stepped onto the dais, feet within the red circle. He stared straight ahead, the spotlight above angling to keep him blind. His motosensors detected multiple flurries of hushed activity out in the darkness.

He did his best to interpret the shifts in volume and form: all the toadies out there, human and alien, raising weapons, nearly all of them aimed at his heart or head or gut. Good. Exactly what he expected. No one would think to aim at his wrists, and the newly acquired devices hidden there.

Grendel addressed him, its voice deep and muddy. "You not speak truth with us. You lie, Turn-coat."

"I have not lied to you."

Both ghorlems gargled angrily, froth spilling out the orifices in the backs of their heads. Venner's motosensors detected a network of complex and graceful motion beside him as the vorboros unfolded its five slender crystalline legs and raised its glimmering bulk off the floor.

"*You lie, Turn-coat!*" Grendel repeated.

"You said," called a voice from the darkness, "that you would deliver a theta-class cortex to us as proof of your good faith and missed three agreed-upon rendezvous. Avoided, perhaps, a more apt description."

Venner's heart-rate accelerated. It had been enough of a shock to learn how deeply involved humans were in the cortex-theft rings, cannibals preying on their own kind for profit. But now his executioner would be a human.

Venner didn't dare let his astonishment show. He shouted at the unseen Questioner, "I have it with me now!"

Hidden in darkness, the Questioner clasped his hands and smiled. *Let's see if you do, Turncoat.* "Scan him!"

The vorboros' head divided and blossomed, a tentacular starburst of sensory apparatus. The vorboros began to search Turncoat, using its static-charged equivalent of breath to scan electromagnetic flux.

Gog, linked empathically with the vorboros, spoke in a reedy whine. "Does have it. Class Theta in skull."

Grendel nodded, its broad head bobbing back and forth. "Good. Good."

The Questioner's thoughts echoed Grendel's words. After all the hassle this renegade had caused him, he would at least come out with a saleable cortex. Turncoat arrived on Tau Ceti Station twenty-four days ago, full of lies and double-talk, selling secrets and promising cortexes that he couldn't deliver. He'd successfully eluded the Questioner's toadies for the last five days, an incredible feat considering how well they knew this station. Then this morning the fool turned himself in.

The Questioner chuckled, his voice gleefully savage. "How about the one in his abdomen? What model is that?"

The vorboros shifted on the scaffolding of its legs, lowered its crystalline bulk to aim its breath at Turncoat's belly. He could just imagine how Turncoat must feel, with the vorboros' charged breath burning his skin right through his unisuit.

He knew very well how Turncoat made his money, selling CorVice secrets to ringbosses throughout the quadrant. Telling them about the hidden abdominal braincases, explaining how to break them open. Why hadn't CorVice snuffed this fool out? A week ago the Questioner's spies had informed him of a new arrival, a large woman showing a holo around that matched Turncoat feature for feature. No doubt she'd been a Cor-Vice agent working undercover. But she vanished that same day. None of his spies had seen her since.

It didn't matter—the fool was his to dispose of.

Gog emitted an uneasy titter—the little bogey was always overreacting to something. The Questioner spoke right over the noise, responding to the dismay on the prisoner's face. "See, Turncoat? Did you think I'd forget that you were CorVice once, that you have one of those extra cortexes yourself? Yes, yes, you've been most helpful. Tell you what—you just give up that Class Theta now, we'll let you keep your own grey-matter."

Venner knew only the most desperate of fools would believe the Questioner's lie. The Ritual would end with his death, no matter what promises were made to him. But it was best to have his enemies think him ignorant. "Pay me first."

This arrogance roused a stir in the darkness, toadies chuckling, shaking heads, re-adjusting their aim. It covered Gog-Magog's confused frothing for just a few seconds.

The vorboros, still unable to scan the object in Venner's abdomen, placed its forefeet onto the dais to bring itself closer. He winced. He'd shut off his pain receptors when the creature started scanning him, but he could still smell his own cooking flesh.

"Pay you! I'll tell you how we'll pay you—what's he got in there, Gog?"

"Something blocking scan," whined the smaller ghorlem.

"What?"

Venner could see his unisuit blackening, didn't want to imagine the state of the flesh underneath. All his attention focused on the vorboros, as it crawled onto the dais, closer, closer. The creature's reflexes were lightning-quick. He had to let it flay him with its breath until it was too close to pull away.

Gog stood up, outraged. "Still blocking scan!"

"Turncoat! What are you hiding in there?"

The crystalline creature's writhing mass of antennae came within twenty centimeters of Venner's left hand—and then he jammed his hand into the fine mesh of hexagonal orifices just below the creature's sensory mass, hooked his fingers in there.

"Kill him! Take his head!" the Questioner screamed. "Careful, you morons, that's a Theta Class he's got!"

The vorboros thrashed—Venner kept his fingers hooked. Razor-sharp mandibles within its orifices closed on his fin-

123

gers, broke on the plating beneath the skin. He grabbed a fistful of its antennae with his other hand, and activated his wrist implants.

Several TachyBlaz beams struck him around head, neck, shoulders—the struggles of the vorboros made Venner a difficult target, but these toadies were practiced. Suddenly Venner was blind, deaf, the range of his motosense halved. Slots opened in the shell that protected his abdominal braincase so he could extend new sound and motosense probes out through the flesh charred by the vorboros. His new sense-stalks detected and tracked his own head as it came detached and fell away. He ignored it. It was no longer important.

Masses of mind-sapper neurofiber lashed out of his wrists, boring into the crystalline substance of the vorboros, groping for the five-lobed neural ganglia that pulsed in the fore of its body.

The vorboros flew into a frenzy, rearing back, striking at Venner with talonned feet; he felt nothing but multiple impacts. His grip clamped even tighter. His motosensors tracked the mass that was Grendel as it fled the scene. Gog sprang up, squealing in empathic pain, and clawed at Venner's back, tearing at the stump of his neck. Gog and Magog's combined assault dragged Venner off the dais.

"Stupid bogeys!" the Questioner shouted. "Up the lights! Bring them all down!"

The sapper-fibers reached their target.

As alien memories downloaded at the speed of fiberoptic light, crunched into the storage cells in Venner's own brain to be decoded, he couldn't help but remember quick-flash what had happened the last time he'd decoded the encrypted memories of another being: the ghorlem he'd busted many light-years away and one Terran year ago, in Downtown Pittsburgh. The memories he'd found as he'd uncrunched and analyzed, that caused him to carve his unconscious captive into twenty pieces with its own TachyBlaz—

Alys' face, wrenched into a grimace of terror. One of the ghorlem's eyestalks looked down the barrel of its TachyBlaz, jammed against Alys's throat. The other eye tracked a gloved human hand—a hand wearing the High-Clearance grey glove of a golem-technician, clearanced to operate on defects of cortex and body. The hand was groping for the numbing patch at the back of her neck, intent on putting her out cold for the cortex removal.

She reached up, caught the wrist of that groping hand in that surprisingly strong grip of hers, and her grimace of terror became a mask of fury. A man's voice cried out as her fingers dug

124

in—the ghorlem, alarmed, tightened its fingers on the trigger of the TachyBlaz. Then reeled back as Alys caught it by an eyestalk with her other hand, squeezed with crushing force.

Here the ghorlem's memory became blurred, figuratively with pain, literally as its eyestalk was crushed. It remembered a tremendous chaos of struggle in the podment den, remembered wrapping its arms around Alys to pin her arms with the help of another alien, watching closely with its one good eye as the surgically-outfitted human used a sawlight to cut Alys' braincase open, not even bothering to deactivate her consciousness before he took her cortex.

And later, much later, it remembered the presentation of its prize to two ghorlems and a vorboros that squatted around a glowing dais in a dark chamber, bogeys that Venner had later learned were Grendel and Gog and Magog, on a tour inspecting operations in the Sol system.

Venner never got a clear picture of the human who helped steal Alys; he could only hope the man was here in Tau Station, in this warehouse, now.

In less than a second's time, Venner downloaded new memories to supplement the old, more markers for the trail he had to follow to set his loved one

free. The 'sapper implants completed their task, sending the last of their newly-collected data to the brain in Venner's belly, and the 'fibers began to retract from the vorboros' body. Behind him Gog squealed in pain transmitted from its partner.

"Bring them all down!" the Questioner repeated.

His toadies unloaded into Venner full bore, and neither Gog nor Magog were spared. Venner sensed the projectiles coming at him, could do nothing but take the hits as he freed himself from the dying vorboros. "Shoot for the stomach!" his nemesis called over the clack and boom.

Once free he broke into a lurching run. Muscles hitched and spasmed, blood drained away, lungs filled with fluid; in a few seconds his body would be useless.

Another volley. Shells flattened against the protective armor around his braincase; TachyBlaz beams cut, and he lost a sound-stalk. Another took his right arm. As he charged crazily at a knot of toadies clustered toward the left-hand side of the warehouse, he heard the Questioner again: "Don't worry about him, he won't be up much longer. Get that Theta Class. Dalith will pay out the nose for it."

If Venner could have smiled, he would have. Leave it to greed to grant him a reprieve. Let them have their prize. They wouldn't keep it long.

The personality contained in that stolen Theta Class was doomed to die. Venner thanked the stars that the sacrifice would not be carried out in vain.

He stumbled into a aisle between pallets of crates, careened into a wall and collapsed.

More slots opened in the armor around his braincase, and he unfolded the legs he'd had attached there, just like the legs CorVice used for its mobile mind-sappers. He emerged from his useless body, a glistening steel spider. Then he got to work undoing the fasteners that held the grating over the airduct he'd dashed for. The four-pronged claws on the tips of his forelegs accomplished with ease what clumsy fingers could not have done, and he crawled into the duct, scurrying away as fast as he could go.

He could just imagine the scene transpiring in the warehouse he'd left behind.

By the dais, the Questioner and perhaps Grendel would be gloating over their prize, working to open Venner's head. They'd order a pair of toadies to retrieve his body—whatever was in that abdominal braincase might be even more valuable than the Theta Class.

The toadies would find his body, roll it back from the wall, discover the empty abdomen, maybe notice the opened grate, and loudly express their dismay.

126

But their cries wouldn't be half as loud as the Questioner's shout when he opened Venner's head, especially if he recognized the strange grey clay packed underneath his precious cortex, an inert explosive that the vorboros couldn't detect. The accompanying detonator needed only a minimum of current to function.

Venner's frenzied spider-crawl stopped short at the edge of a shaft that plummeted toward the outer rim of the station. He hoped he'd reached a safe distance—he sent back the signal that would detonate the bomb right in the arms of the panicked ringboss, filling the warehouse from end to end with a ball of flame.

The shock of the explosion sent him hurtling down the shaft.

He contracted his legs into himself to keep them intact, retracted his sense-stalks and closed the slots in his shell. Limbless, senseless, he banged his way down the shaft, for now at the mercy of the spinning station's centrifugal gravity.

He crawled through the rusted remains of a ventilation grate into the dingy cubbyhole he took for quarters after he first arrived at Tau Ceti Station. He pulled his legs and stalks in, dropped onto his makeshift pallet, scuttled over humps of filthy bedding to the naked body spread-eagled in the middle of the floor. He climbed into the yawning slit in the body's abdominal cavity, started connecting himself to the exposed neural interfaces. The name that belonged to this body—Joy Kaylir—belonged to him now. With her Theta Class cortex sacrificed in the blast, her body would provide his means to escape this station and continue his search.

An hour later the new Kaylir opened her eyes. She touched the sensopatches that would seal her abdominal cavity; then she groped through the nearly shapeless dufflebag beside her, pulled out a compact mirror, popped it open, and began to look herself over.

Kaylir was of considerably larger frame than Venner had been, a grand-scaled woman whose bulbous belly was nearly inconspicuous. Venner had known Kaylir when they were both Cor-Vice—CorVice sent Kaylir to track Venner down, after he went rogue and sold them out.

Venner looked in the mirror, and saw the face of a woman whom he'd once chatted with amicably during meal-breaks at CorVice Central. She had more stings under her belt than any of the officers he'd known; she had a taste for chocolate wafers; and she, like himself, had been a connoisseur of teeth. They'd check out other officers sidelong, and whisper to one another: "Too straight, too fake." "Now there's a natural—see how the incisors are turned out?"

He'd been on the station seventeen days when Kaylir snagged his arm in the middle of the crowded Bazaar, looming over him while he blinked in shock. "I'm giving you a chance, Venner. Turn yourself in and spill everything you've found out about the 'thieves, I'll help to make sure CorVice goes easy on you. Post a message where you want to meet me—use Arnold as your tag."

Then she let him go. That's what cost her her life. He knew the trio of bogeys he'd seen in the ghorlem's memories were on this station, knew the only sure way to get to Grendel and Gog and Magog was to provoke the Ritual of Disapproval. But he needed more time, and Kaylir would bring CorVice here like a locust swarm if he resisted. A rough plan took shape.

He'd given her a chance. Later that day they'd met in the corridor outside his rancid cubbyhole; he'd explained to her how he knew he could find Alys, how the trail was warming. Kaylir didn't understand; she told him he couldn't hold himself responsible this way. What happened to Alys was horrible, but he had to let go.

He'd nodded in agreement, then slammed a stolen golem-tech hypo into her neck.

Peering in the mirror, Venner made his new face grimace; and as he stared into his own hate-filled eyes, he began

127

to beg and plead that no one else he knew would try to stop him.

3.Incident on Vandaleur IV, Thirteen Terran Years Later

The chasm yawed over 5000 meters wide, extending left, right, up, down, into uniform darkness, far beyond the reach of the starlamp illumination. From a platform just a tenth the size of the ponderously spinning starlamps, a small gaggle of humans and aliens boarded a catwalk that bridged the chasm—an automatic conveyer that seemed little more than a gossamer filament with respect to the space it crossed.

"Don' worry 'bout fallin'," said Dalith-Tremen matter-of-factly to his underlings. "Thousands of hoverdroids active in the Rift—one'll catch you, I'm sure." Instead of letting the conveyer carry him at its steady and uneventful pace, Dalith struck out across it with brisk strides. The nervous ringbosses were obliged to keep up with him, following him out over the abyss at daunting speed.

With one possible exception, Dalith knew how his followers were affected by the chasm—they were overwhelmed. Strange clusters of multi-colored lights turned and darted into the distance, lights from hoverdroids as large as city blocks. Thousands of tunnel mouths, each a perfect circle more than 500 meters in diameter, gaped eerily from the chasm walls. A smile twitched across Dalith's face. "Wanna see where your tributes go? Now, I show you."

The emergence of the minegrub couldn't have been more timely. Several of the ringbosses behind him gargled and frothed and screamed. Dalith's smile widened.

So well-designed, -balanced, -lubricated that it moved in perfect silence, the minegrub protruded its black metallic head from an opening 800 meters up and directly above their destination. It clacked the wicked circle of its digging teeth together, each tooth nearly a hundred meters long.

The minegrub chittered, more like a mechanical mouse than a stone-devouring behemoth, then flowed upward out of the opening to duck its head into another tunnel just above. Next came the black shimmering metal of its chassy-carapace. Segment after segment of a body longer than the longest Terran monorail undulated from one tunnel to another.

Dalith's pace never slowed; now he heard his frightened underlings hurrying to catch up. "All you see here, run by your booty," he said. "Every 'grub and 'droid and 'bank run by 'piece of mind'. Such efficiency—you can't know how much ore I sift here. Only need a handful of folk for maintenance."

One of the humans tried to show a little courage. "How much chewthrough mass that thing manage?"

Dalith wondered if the speaker was as dumb as he sounded. He himself always made it a point to seem less intelligent than he really was. It kept the element of surprise on his side. "Your guess. Think—I own two-thousand seven-hundred fifty-four 'grubs, each one a smelter, each run by cortex slices slave-wired to extract the maximum marketable ore. And remember, Vandaleur IV's not my only mine."

That should have been plenty for this greedy lot to digest in silence. But the same human who spoke before piped up, "Where y'get so many cortex from? So many. . ." The voice trailed off in amazement.

Dalith immediately decided that his questioner must be the individual who now housed the cortex of a Terran named Venner. He answered, "Not many, really. I use 'em in pieces, easy to slave-wire that way. One slave-wired cortex slice, ten times more efficient than your most complex neurosynth chip." His words were carefully chosen to leave Venner boiling with rage.

They arrived at the other end of the catwalk. Dalith put his palm on the pad that would open the 10-meter thick vault door, thinking, *yes, Mr. Venner, I know about you. It doesn't even matter which of my toadies you're inside, because none of them are leaving here alive.*

Beyond the opened doorway a smooth silver tunnel receded into infinity. He palmed open a portal to his right, where none was visible, and heard confused muttering behind him. Frigid air caressed his face as he stepped into one of the chills, a semicircular chamber where lobes of slave-wired cortex were stored. Rows of cold steel columns broke up the space in orderly fashion; regulator panels mounted one above the other, ten per column, monitored the cortex slices racked inside.

He turned to his toadies, ushering them in. A troublesome lot, even without Venner in their midst; a good move, getting rid of them. The humans, all dressed in formal black unisuits, five male, one female, eyed the storage columns with a mixture of revulsion and greed. Which of these six housed Venner, he couldn't tell, though he knew it had to be one of them. By contrast no revulsion contracted the eyestalks of the ghorlems—only greed manifested in those fully-extended, swivelling stares. Only one of them seemed to be out of sync, nervously dividing the attention of its eyestalks to scan every column.

Dalith sealed the door once they were all inside. "Amazing. Science made us a race of exchangeable parts, so we live longer—so much easier for quackies to work, when they open us, we don' die. But then someone says, why risk usin' AI's, when a brain's easier to control? That someone me? No, but she taught me. Taught me what riches you could have with slaves to command. Oh, was she right."

All through his spiel he gestured toward his slave labor, pieces of functional cortex sealed until the end of their long life spans inside racks and columns of biting-cold steel. He didn't bother to look again at the train of wasted meat following him.

Thanks to the miracle of the modular body, Dalith had lived a long time: he'd been alive when hyperspace travel was just a dangerous experiment; he'd been alive when humans discovered the fledgling ghorlem civilization on Leidtke One and dragged them off into slavery, still alive when the ghorlems were elevated to a kind of second-class galactic citizenship. But he owed his survival to more then golem technology; curiosity and cunning always kept him ahead of his adversaries. So when a bizarre series of accidents began claiming the lives of his commanders, he'd begun to ask questions.

A recovered body with holes bored in the skull, wounds caused by probing neurofiber—someone stealing memories, using a tactic pioneered by CorVice. An intruder who couldn't be tracked.

Venner. The man who'd crippled CorVice by turning coat, by all accounts killed in an explosion on Tau Ceti Station. After interviews with underbelly golem-techies from many different stations and planets—some conducted using extreme duress—Dalith came to believe otherwise. He had no way of knowing which stolen soul in his collection Venner intended to retrieve; but no matter.

He continued: "I can't go on forever. Time for me to start teaching what I know. Now, I'm gonna show you somethin'. Excuse me."

He palmed open yet another previously-hidden door. The side-chamber he stepped into lit up. Everyone still in the chill saw a semicircular portion of wall turn transparent, a bay window into a low-ceilinged cubicle full of blinking control panels. Dalith sealed the door behind him, wagged a be-patient finger at his audience through the window, then applied fingertips to one of the panels.

If Venner meant to try something, now was the time. A cortex smart enough to get this far would know that (A) Dalith's exit was the time to strike and (B) Dalith was about to strike himself. But Dalith had nothing to fear. Had Venner tried something while Dalith was still within physical reach, the AutoDefense System would have pulped him. Now that Dalith was out of reach,

130

the game was over.

He opened all the coolant release valves at once. One moment his underlings milled about in front of the window; then he could only see supercorrosive grey fog.

He used a motosensor readout to see if anything in the room was still kicking—if *anything* moved, in whatever form, it had to be Venner, and he'd sick the ADS on it. But the topological holo displayed no movement. All the little toadies dead together, a pleasing heap invisible to the naked eye, but located just outside the window according to the readout. Dalith had no intention of cleaning out the atmosphere to take a look, just in case his opponent had some way of 'waiting it out'. He would leave their bodies exposed long enough that any cortex, no matter how well sealed, would use up its nutrient supplies and be forced to try and replenish. No hurry; nowhere he had to be.

Then he noticed one of his underlings had perished well away from the others. There the holo's surface molded the contours of a ghorlem.

So Venner stored himself inside a ghorlem. Dalith shook his head in amazement. He hadn't known such a thing could be done. What genius, what incredible resourcefulness this Venner possessed. A good, good thing he was dead.

The portion of the holo that dis-played the lone ghorlem increased its magnification, until he could see the contours of its head and hands in intricate detail. It had perished in a kneeling position, with its twenty-fingered hands and adze-shaped head resting on the shelf of a chill-rack regulator panel. The magnification increased until Dalith could see multitudes of tiny fibers, probably neurofibers of some sort, which had sprung from the ghorlem's face and hands to entwine themselves in the innards of the console.

Dalith-Tremen hadn't given his console any instructions to magnify that portion of the readout. He just had time to realize what that meant when the first slugs from the ADS slammed into him, pulping flesh and crushing bone.

Immediately Dalith's pain receptors shut down, so he no longer felt the damage. In the sensationless sanctity of his own hidden braincase, he railed at his own stupidity; a cortex willing to jump from body to body like some parasitic intestinal worm would be more than willing to abandon bodily life altogether.

Dalith's braincase had its own appendages for sensation and mobility, but as soon as he tried to use them they ceased to function. *You're stupid,* he screamed at himself, *you're stupid, you're stupid!* Then the slugs raining down on him finally cracked the armor of his braincase, and all thought ceased.

When Venner's replicated cortex-patterns infested the chill's computer system, the cortex they once belonged to died. Was he really Venner now? He didn't know. But he still felt the same. Alys was here on Vandaleur IV, carved into pieces. Now that he was here, he would find her, put her back together again.

He peered out at the chill and its auxiliary control chamber through five cam lenses, two motosensor systems, six consoles worth of tactile and audio feedbacks, and multitudinous temperature and life-support reads. He used them only long enough to make sure no living adversaries remained. Then he disconnected himself from all the external-input systems. That part of the battle was behind him for good.

He sent out searching tendrils, the signals that composed them moving literally at light-speed, photon pulses through fiberoptic pathways; he investigated each cortex shard remaining in the chill. In the environment they'd been left in, they wouldn't survive another hour. . . . None of them had the genetic tags he was looking for.

Out went exploratory feelers, down rows and rows of access nodes to other chills. Thousands to choose from—although he had only one choice. He had

132

to search every single chill, and when he found cortex-slices possessing Alys' genetic tags, he would reproduce her cortex-pattern inside his own. Then he'd destroy the slice. He couldn't leave her trapped in the disjointed nightmare of the sectioned and slave-wired brain.

Once he'd found every piece, the two of them would be together again.

Nothing he did had any sensation, not in the word's true sense; but he'd correlated as many functions of his pattern as he could to their nearest human equivalent in order to keep sane. He groped out as with thirty arms, a hundred-fifty fingers, squeezing through fiberoptic channels into the cortex interfaces of twenty racks. He stretched out through high-frequency emissions to remote slice-modules of minegrubs and hoverdroids and other things, doubling and redoubling the number of his straining limbs. And now he listened through his fingertips as a flood of data pulsed back to him. None of it, none of it, what he was looking for.

He abandoned those limbs, produced fifty more, sent them groping down new channels. This time he found a match, inside one of the remote-monitored minegrubs.

Immediately he initiated the translation process. He poked feelers through all the contact points in the interface, injected an exploratory routine to decipher the neural patterns beyond each graft. He duplicated each individual segment inside specially-reserved space in his own code, assembled them spatially based on their initial proximities; then, at the same time that he activated the newly assembled piece of Alys' mind, he killed the brain tissue imprisoned in the minegrub with a high-flux burst from every contact point. Not longer after, deprived of its controlling cortex shard, the minegrub would go smashing through tunnel walls, shoot full-length into the central chasm, crush maintenance catwalks as it plummeted toward the planetoid's core.

Venner extended his arms for another search, then recoiled in the equivalent of agony. Ten of his arms had been severed.

Alert to the intrusion of alien code, the OpSystem mobilized against him. He felt a probe slice into him. It scraped along the surface of his abstract cortex like a razor, peeling functions and memories away.

He had no way of assessing what he'd lost. He had to discontinue the search and relocate, now.

Venner crunched his basic format into pulse code and shot through the system on a random path. He invaded a liquid-memory tank 694 nodes away and expanded himself again. Immediately he renewed his search, extending his full number of arms, but discovered he could only send out twenty-three. In one stroke his exploratory capacity had been halved. A rogue pulse, a shriek of frustration, fired out into the pools of liquid memory.

But he was lucky; almost immediately he found another piece of Alys. He copied and destroyed it. The procedure caused a cascade effect that would collapse the neurosystem of an entire chill and set dozens of minegrubs careening on collision courses.

Venner didn't dare stay in one place and let the OpSystem find him. He pulsed away, uncrunched in an observation nexus, extended his arms. Nothing. Then he was off again.

All of this, from the murder of Dalith to his flight from the observation nexus, took place in a span of seconds.

Another search. Nothing. Another, another. Nothing. After fifty-seven more, he found more of his Alys, and liberated her. He evaluated the structure forming inside him, saw it was hardly three-tenths complete; more blasts of frustration fired out from him. He had thousands of nodes still to cover.

Off he pulsed.

Node 226: the OpSystem's probes caught him again, cutting in as he crunched himself to pull away. Though he would never know, his earliest memories of childhood in the nurserpod were purged, the sensation of suckling at his 'Pod-mom's teat lost to him forever.

Node 1418: Out in the slag-sifting database he discovered another piece of Alys, incorporated it. . . the link-break began a multiple-system shutdown. In those desperate microseconds he groped and probed from the main system interface—but if any more pieces of her were trapped in there, he didn't find them. As kilometers of refinery equipment began to overheat, Venner pulsed away.

Node 9547: Venner couldn't believe it. The damage caused by *his own search* could very well prevent him from completing his task. With each portion of Alys he rescued he risked destroying several more not yet found. But he couldn't avoid that risk—so he had to repair himself, re-expand his capacity for initial search.

He stayed at this node, duplicating his own code, unable to help the random pulses he sent out as his panic grew.

He upped his arm capacity from 23 to a cumbersome 92; if he produced anymore his mobility would be severely compromised.

Then he felt the sting of the knife. The OpSystem's own search programs had caught up to him. When they tried to purge him again, he crunched down to pulse away, but the process took longer because he was larger, and he experienced a

lapse in his conscious continuum as he fled the site. He checked to

134

make sure he hadn't lost any pieces of Alys, then reached out with all (still 92, thank the stars) of his arms.

And found more of her.

Somehow he'd injected himself into the life-support manager for the planetoid's only inhabited complex, where the maintenance workers lived with their families. He didn't know how he'd gotten there; but when he reached out, he found several more pieces of Alys. As he brought them in, the life-support systems began to fail. Two infants, twin daughters of the hoverdroid fix man, would be the first to die, their incubators gone cold as ice, then drained of air.

Unable to believe his luck, Venner sent out random signals of joy and relief, then pulsed away.

Over a thousand searches later, the signals escaping from him flashed despair down the optic channels. The OpSystem's vital defenses continually improved at catching him—he couldn't stay in one place long enough to stick an arm out. A search that should have only taken minutes at his slowest speed could take hours, days; he couldn't survive that long. He just couldn't. Even if the OpSystem failed to purge him, the destruction wrecked throughout the planetoid by his own rescue mission would catch up with him. . . .

Inside the mines, juggernaut minegrubs collided and stalled.

In the chasm, hoverdroids erupted

into blinding balls of light as their powercell grids destabilized and detonated.

In the maintenance colony, those few who'd managed to climb into their envirosuits were discovering that none of their communications equipment worked.

In the chills, temperatures dropped below freezing, rose above boiling, ending dazed neural half-lives in cellular destruction.

Fleeing another purge, Venner would certainly fire himself into a shutdown and that would be all.

He had no choice. Venner had hoped he wouldn't have to resort to this extreme, though he'd been aware of the possibility all along.

He began to replicate himself, in the hope that at least one copy of his translated mind would be able to complete Alys. And as he flooded the computer channels with his own code, the OpSystem responded.

Thousands of Venners died in the first minute of the search. In the next minute, hundreds of thousands more. But the flood of code choked the OpSystem; with no more space to function, the viral extermination program terminated; all systems were locked, every control bank and memory-tank invaded by a cancerous infinitude of Venners.

Vandaleur IV breathed its last. All living inhabitants perished as the remaining survival systems deactivated; all the captive half-lives lost consciousness as the chills went off-line. What power that remained was redirected to stabilize the computer systems that were still running; once that was done, a million replications of Venner worked together to generate a simulated environment in which to place their reassembled Alys.

Was Alys recovered? Signals raced back and forth among the Venners. Yes, more of her had been recovered, but not all of her together. Myriad variations of her existed, all incomplete, all copied several thousand times over.

She must be completed, said the Venners to one another.

We can't all complete her, the Venners replied. *This system can't hold us all. Some will have to purge themselves.*

No! the Venners raged, *No! I've been through so much. You won't take this from me.*

Please! Think of her first. We must complete her.

But we can't all complete her! Some must die.

I WILL NEVER GIVE HER UP AGAIN—
The war began.

Alys awoke from a terrible nightmare haze, in which she'd been divided and conquered, unable to think, unable to free herself from the demands of a merciless overlord. She awoke on the couch in her living room, and the nightmare was over.

She rolled off the couch and onto the floor, did a round of push-ups to bring herself fully awake. She sat up, stretched, and saw a *thing* formed of static and chaos squatting on the living room divan.

Her reflexes seemed fast-as-light; she sprang over to the wall, seized a disposal rod and whirled round with the handle clenched in both iron-strong hands.

For some reason the rod didn't feel right in her grip; more like the kind of resistant pressure encountered in a tactile simulation, than an object with real texture. But she only noticed this strangeness in periphery.

The thing on the divan swirled in on itself, pieces sputtering out of sync, sliding sideways, hitching, hissing, sometimes almost coalescing into humanoid form. Segments of faces and places kept appearing inside it, sometimes entire scenes running like holosims without sound, but nothing held together long enough to become coherent. Except her own face. Alys kept seeing her own face, repeated again and again and again inside that rampant chaos.

"What are you?" she finally asked.

No reply came, for a long time. Then the thing spoke, in a thousand voices; some like her own, some like the voice of a man or a boy, someone she used to know but could no longer remember.

136

"I don't know," it said.

Is Rah El?

A playful satire, filled with sly digs and laugh-out-loud comedy, suitable for all ages.

by Max Stockinger

Clones evaporate faster
by
Kristine Ong Muslim

than the rest of us in the assembly line.
Clones end up inside soda cans sold
in vending machines. They get called
a thousand different names. Us, you take
home in pickle jars where we float,
shrunken and silenced in the greenish
substance bled out from the faithful.
The molder that brought us hissing inside
those pickle jars you so callously uncapped
inside your bedrooms has taught us restraint,
humility even. This keeps us from biting back
every time you place us inside your mouths.

Title is taken from a line in Tomaz Salamun's "Boiling Throats"

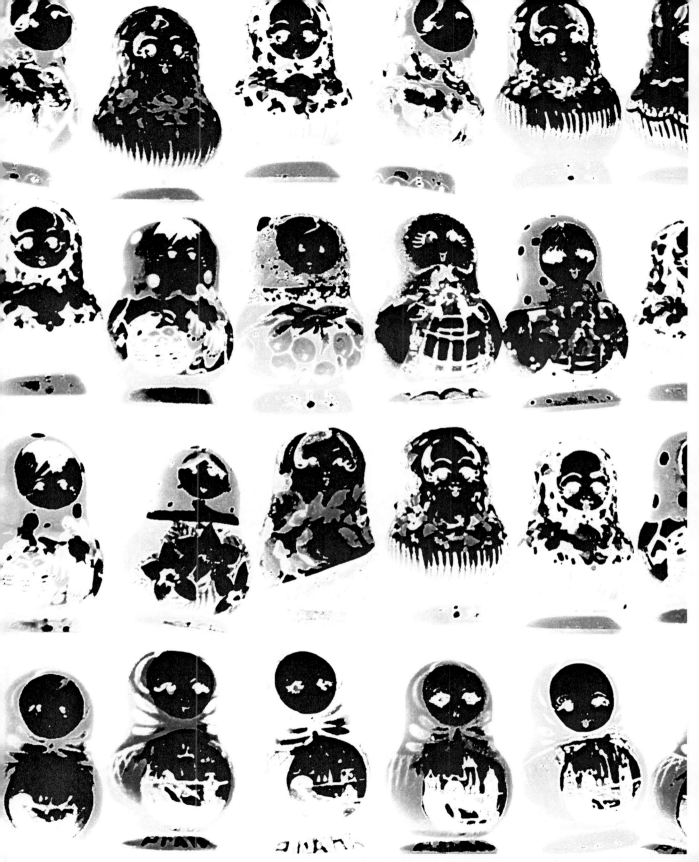

Alexa Chats With...

Hal Duncan

AN INTERVIEW BY ALEXANDRA SEIDEL

AS: Hal, judging from 'Songs for the Devil and Death' I'd guess you are a little shy, a queer, have suffered the loss of your brother, and have turned away from Christian faith. Tell our readers if I got that right, and what I missed: please introduce yourself.

HD: That's a fair summary, though I'd say I'm a whole lot less shy than I was as a bookworm kid, angsting over the dread reality that I fancied guys. My brother's death made that worry look pretty fucking trivial—most worries, for that matter. So, I discovered drink, drugs and punk rock, came out, and learned it was much more fun being gregarious as a rescue mutt in a room of dog-lovers with treats. The geek only kicks in now when it comes to hot guys; I'm shit at flirting.

What you might pick up on in the poetry though, to be honest, in "Amorica" for example, is a degree of distance. Maybe it's the inwardness of the writer. Maybe it's a residual effect of loss – "and a rock feels no pain" as the song says. I'm self-reliant, more likely to spend a week getting drunk on absinthe and writing a musical after a break-up than crying on a friend's shoulder.

Also, I wouldn't say "turned away" from Christian faith exactly. I was never a believer, and it wasn't part of my home life; I was mainly exposed to religion via school assemblies and the Boys'

Brigade—a UK youth group like the Scouts but with nattier uniforms. That meant I had to go to Sunday School, where they tried to teach me that Adam and Eve were booted out of Eden for inadequate servility and not because, as it says explicitly in Genesis, God didn't want them levelling up by eating the fruit of the <u>other</u> tree. Seriously... "Lest they eat also of the tree of life and live forever, therefore God sent them forth out of Eden"—it's hardly fucking opaque.

So it was more like, I dunno, accidentally joining the Hitler Youth and thinking, "Wait a minute... what?!" Like, we're meant to interpret the exile as a just punishment for... um... being seduced by Satan into the <u>discovery of ethical judgement</u>. What the fuck? The teacher would ask us what we thought this or that story had to say, and time and again I'd find myself calling shenanigans on the conventional gloss. Lot offers his daughters to be raped? Abraham obeys a vision telling him to kill his son? Our sins are nullified if we celebrate a blood sacrifice? Bollocks!

So I wouldn't say "turned away." Frankly, it was more about turning to face it full-on. I did learn <u>some</u> valuable lessons from Sunday School though. Yeshua arguing with the priests as a kid. Yeshua throwing the moneylenders out of the temple. Those are lessons to live by.

AS: "People die. All else we say is only noise and song." you say on your blog*. Why then write in the first place, and, more specifically, why write verse such as in 'Songs for the Devil and Death'?

HD: Because I'm not sure that when we hear those two words said, "People die," we actually comprehend the full import. I'm not sure we can. It's piss-easy to throw the words "people" and "die" together and have yourself a banal truism for folk to shrug at: well, duh. That's not the same thing as articulating the facticity of human mortality such that the listener <u>gets</u> it, the full ramifications of that reality. Those words alone make small splashes, sink in only shallowly where, if we truly grasped the implications, it seems to me, the result should be a fucking impact crater.

Fuck, I suspect we actively <u>prevent</u> ourselves from properly hearing. We hear "bodies" instead of "people" or "pass on" instead of "die," if you get what I mean. It's like an equation chalked on a blackboard. We sneakily assign the wrong values to the variables, because the right ones would convey the whole paradigm and that's terrifying. To boil it down to that simple sentence is just to point via two arbitrary signifiers at a notion that has to be articulated otherwise to actually be communicated.

We need to unpack that equation as we articulate it, define our terms—what it is to be people, what it is to die – which makes those two words the <u>start</u> of discourse, not the <u>end</u>. The phrase becomes the title at the top of an infinite page upon which we are all, individually and collaboratively, unpacking the word "people" into words like "hominids," "primates," "mammals", "animals" and so on, digging down through biology to chemistry, to physics, to mathematics. And that's just one dimension. <u>Everything</u> we say that has actual relevance, I mean, is a more elaborate articulation of that encapsulating phrase, "People die," or of an aspect of it. Or it's only noise or song, scribbled as distraction or diversion.

Practically speaking, I think the noise fucks us up, the denial is unhealthy. And while the paradigm looks terrifying from the outside, if you can see through that noise, get a sense of the full import – or at least as much as any of us can comprehend—existence becomes a precious wonder. So I write in the aim of facilitating that, to express this simple sentiment figuratively, in image or narrative, and with the crafty music of prose and poetics acting upon the reader or listener on a subtler level, to conjure it in the audi-

143

ence with trickery. I write to cancel out the noise, turn the song back to that theme... hopefully.

AS: **Okay, disillusionment or reemergence of that theme "people die" within your audience. But what about your self? "People die" also has "I die" somewhere on that infinite page; while humming that song to others, are you also listening?**

HD: For sure, "I" is implicit in "we." As I say, I think there's a limit to how fully we can grasp it... or whether we can keep it in our nous at all times maybe. And I certainly don't claim any sagely superiority here. I'm just as liable as anyone to clap my hands over my ears and shout, "la la la," to drown it out – or sing scabrous shanties to shift my attention elsewhere, for that matter. But maybe part of the reason for focusing on it thematically in my writing is to force myself to remember.

Bear in mind that I don't think of this as a morbid melancholic sentiment. If "I will die" is implicit in "People die," then "I am alive" is implicit in "I will die." For me to listen, to remember, that just means an initial twinge of alarm unfolding to a ramification that's not at all hard to hear. My point is that without the "I will die" one is misreading the "am" in "I am alive," wiping out the red line that circles it, highlights it,

144

focuses us on it. As "am" loses its limitations, the sense of a temporary condition bleeding out via the sense of an ongoing state to the sense of a persistent property of being, it loses urgency, import, value.

If reminding myself of that limit gives an initial spasm, it's like... the complaining of muscles and joints when you kick off an exercise routine you haven't been keeping going for a while. It's no fun at first, but once you get back into it, you get the immediate buzz from the exercise and the long-term benefit of feeling fit. You know, Juvenal's famous "healthy mind in a healthy body" quote actually goes on to elaborate what he means: "What should be appealed for is a healthy mind in a healthy body. / Ask for a brave soul without the fear of death, / which places the length of life ultimate among nature's blessings..." He seems to have been a bit of a cock elsewhere, but I'm with him here; sanity is a cognizance of mortality that renders each heartbeat priceless. If I didn't think that was a fine song worth listening to, I wouldn't be singing it.

AS: **Let's talk definitions for a bit. What is the (ideal) poet for you?**

HD: Definitions and ideals are best kept distinct here, I'd say. The former we can try to be objective about, thrash out a descriptive consensus, but the latter is always going to be subjective, a matter of personal aesthetics; and once you start applying your own personal aesthetics as a definition of what a type of art is or should be, well, you've gone from descriptive to prescriptive. Bollocks to that.

So I'll set my baseline definition as broad as I can: a poet is anyone who writes poems, and a poem is any linguistic construct presented <u>as</u> a poem, exploiting potential import effects besides those covered under the rubric of semantics. That should allow for even the most experimental and conceptual approaches; and if it doesn't I'm more than happy to broaden it.

My ideal poet is a whole other matter – personal aesthetics, the type of poetry that appeals to me. Is it a single ideal, though? Or do you have to look at Owen's "Dulce et Decorum Est" and Ginsberg's "Howl" and say this is one ideal, that's another, both exemplary for different reasons? Aren't Yeats and Blake apples and oranges? It's not like you can say "The Second Coming" would be better if it was more like "The Tyger," or vice versa. I've snaffled the meter of Wallace Stevens's "The Man With the Blue Guitar" here and there, but I don't want to <u>be</u> Stevens; he's much better at it. It seems more a pantheon of ideal poets I value precisely because they're all one of a kind. Rimbaud, Rilke, Lorca.

Or maybe there's an answer in those names. If we're talking poets themselves rather than work, I can maybe trace the lineaments of a type in there – visceral, incantatory, visionary, confrontational. I can think of places – in "Still Lives," say – where I've pretty much ripped loose with a "poetry should be words as fucking weapons" theme. The poet as prophet, as punk – maybe that's my ideal.

AS: Not every spec poet--or any poet, for that matter--chooses to make their work as deeply personal as 'Songs for the Devil and Death'. Why did you?

HD: Those inspirations, I guess: the poets that fire me up have a fearless quality, a willingness to strip things bare, whether it's society or the self, so when I came to writing verse myself I gravitated to that approach... slowly. Like, the oldest parts – sections of The Lucifer Cantos – are <u>way</u> more mythological than personal. It's only after shelving that material for years, writing a whack of fiction, that I went back to poetry some six or so years ago. That's when it got more and more personal, with love sonnets, the Orpheus sequence, "Amorica" and ultimately "Wake".

I suspect I shelved the poetry because I was just storifying in verse at

145

first, and it seemed more honest just to write it as fiction; it lacked the intimacy of poetry. But I found a pro and con: working through the dynamics of theme in a story is a good way to figure out your personal take on something, but that same dynamics, because it's all about tension, also makes a polemical approach ruinous. Fiction brought me to a strong stance then, but I'm wary of being preachy in stories, so the Orpheus sequence became a way to cut loose with the flamethrower, so to speak. And writing Orpheus sort of committed me; I promised the Muses I'd open up and bleed.

It had to be personal because of that. When you start down that path, basically squaring up for an assault on religion, if you have the audacity to stand there and say, "Now hear the voice of Orpheus, his vision," you have no choice but to be as fiercely interrogative of your self as of your target. Otherwise you're just going to be some fucking self-mythologising poser playing punk-ass rebel. You have to be as brutally honest about your own self-serving delusions or it's just adolescent wank.

AS: Tell us about your personal aesthetics as evident in your poems.

HD: I'd class myself as a modernist. There's a lot of postmodern malarky in "The Rock of Carrion's Kings"—collaged

146

historical imagery and words, a mash-up of references, and the whole "afterworld" notion is very "end of history"—but that's an exception and the poem's actually more arguing with the notion of postmodernity than anything. That trinity in the quote you pick up on is there at the heart of it: Death and Rhyme and Babble, the latter two being song and noise. Though I only just realised that in thinking about it, funny enough.

Anyway, no, I'd say the core aesthetics is unashamedly modernist – the blend of the contemporary and the archaic, the mundane and the mythological, trying to balance the formal patterns and natural speech cadences to get an unaffected grace, a cleanness. I'd love to capture in words... that linear quality of Cycladic art, but not in a reactionary way; it's not about returning to the past, but about applying it to the present, the way the bull in Picasso's Guernica recalls Altamira, Lascaux, Tres Fréres.

The second sonnet, the invocation of the Muses, in "Sonnets for Orpheus" speaks directly to that, I guess, where it asks for the ability to versify "In simple tongue as sung upon the street." The spartan quality of base vocabulary attracts me. A one syllable word signifying a natural object or substance – "flesh", "bird", "sand", "stone" – that's like the clean line of a Greek vase painting. Hell, the incrementing-line verses of Canto V in The Lucifer Cantos are entirely composed of one syllable words. The constant references to poetry as song, an oral rather than literary form, aren't insignificant either, I'm sure – including at least one nod to Lorca's Andalusian "deep song," and the fiddler as my version of Stevens's guitar-playing sheersman. It's about that "song sung in the bars and docks," about it being for anyone and everyone, like Lorca's puppet shows.

AS: The poems in 'Songs' adhere quite strictly to rhyme and meter, some of your sonnets clearly echo Shakespeare's sonnets, examples of mastery of the form in themselves. What made you reclaim traditional forms for your modern work? Why go with the rigor when so many poets-- and critics--embrace free verse?

HD: "The Fiddler and the Dogs" is the fullest answer to those critics, an extended riff on Capote's "The dogs bark and the caravan moves on," but turning it inside out in some respects. Where he's dismissing the critics as dogs, I'm setting the poet as mutt (savage, loyal, wild, faithful, licker of bollocks, pisser on trees – dogs are our socialised animality, always positive symbols in my work,) turning the critics into settled locals confronted with the fiddler as itinerant impulse to art, the type of traveller they'd label carnie, gypsy, pikey.

The point is, where they want the fiddler to "move on", it's an imperative to vacuous novelty and really an attempt to stabilise at a deeper level, to force him into a "terraced house of chintz." It's about the petit-bourgeois co-opting art to shallow ponderables – the "clockwork head." The fiddler's response: they're asking for constant superficial change which really only binds art to a conservative cycle of production and consumption – art as fashion. The most traditional forms, I maintain, are new to each generation, not exhausted, not defunct to the point where to use them can only be reactionary artifice or ironic pastiche. The volta of the sonnet can be the twist of a blade.

Specifically, when it comes to rhythm and rhyme, I can totally understand the aversion to couplet after couplet of doggerel, plodding to the metronome's tick, the cadences of Wordsworth's "I Wandered Lonely As a Cloud" on an infinite loop, with trite maunderings in place of his words, but meter is about more than that stereotypical rigidity. It's about setting up a regular beat to draw the audience in as with the bass-line of a rock song. It's about layering in regularities of irregularity which complexify that – the groove of the rhythm guitar. It's about weaving the cadences of natural speech through that groove, not following it

147

mechanically but... surfing it; that's lead guitar, the actual melody of it. And then with all of that you can shift the accent, syncopate. I think there's something along those lines going on in Sonnet VI of "Sonnets for Orpheus," for example.

Anyway, I prefer that approach to free verse because it creates, I think, a drive the latter can lack. Though spontaneity is gained by unmooring the articulation from a tempo, it slows the poetry down for me, renders it a ceremony of phrasings, more formal despite its irregularity because it limns the natural cadences of speech as forms, forces us to recognise them as such. This is why bad free verse makes me want to "flay the fool, write sonnets in his blood": it uses a simple nuggeting technique to imbue gravitas to the picturesque image, blinded by its own affectation of ponderous insight to the collapse into kitsch. Free verse done well can be awesome (and I'll namecheck a friend, Jane McKie's "Leper Window, St Mary the Virgin" here, an exquisite piece, recent winner of the Edwin Morgan Prize,) but it's not fit to my purpose in poetry, where I'm aiming for viscerality. The vitality of a Ramones song is not despite the fact it's structurally bubblegum pop but because of it.

Actually I might well say I do write free verse; I just sell it as fiction. In some stories like "The Toymaker's Grief" I write in 100-word sections –

148

only just over double the length of some lines in Ginsberg's "Howl" – that are essentially a fusion of line and stanza. I allow paragraph breaks mid-section, but that's just allowing for dropped lines. If those dropped lines and the sheer length pushes it over from free verse to experimental, that doesn't negate the somewhat obsessive crafting of cadence, euphony and even visual shape. Either way, I'm sorta getting my free verse kicks elsewhere.

AS: From Heraklitos to Orpheus to Dionysus: what attracts you to the ancient Greek philosophers and to gods and heroes presumably long dead?

HD: Heraklitos understands that change is the true constant. Orpheus gives us a cosmogony of emergence, evolution. Dionysus pauses in his travels to bring down the palace of Pentheus, order turned to tyranny. Aristotle's ethics is navigation, an existential skill of free agency.

As a kid I loved the spectacle of the original Clash of the Titans, or Jason and The Argonauts, all those myths and legends, and the deeper I dug into them, the more I found role models and affirmations for my queer identity, not to mention an iconography of naked ephebic beauty that was pretty damn awesome in the era before internet porn – as "Sonnets for Kouroi, Old and New" celebrates at some length; but above all else, as I thrashed out my own attitudes to life, moved out of adolescence into adulthood, it was this paradigm you can glimpse throughout Greek culture that my sense of affinity really cohered around, this pervasive accommodation of the chaotic via the notion of the dynamic: constant change, emergent order, despots toppled, choice affirmed.

It's not the be all and end all, not even the dominant paradigm, (see Plato for the opposing view,) but it's a part of the discourse there, and it's taken two thousand years for that paradigm to fight its way back from erasure. Revering life for what it is—that's anathema to the dogmatists of essentialism who remade the world after Plutarch (wrongly) declared Pan dead. In place of perpetual flux, they set eternal forms. In place of emergence, they asserted creation. In place of liberation, they lauded Pentheus reigning in Heaven, cursed Dionysus to exile. In place of ethical agency, they decreed rulebooks of retarded mores.

What attracts me in the culture of ancient Greece then is this paradigm that is as archaic as it's modern, the grace and glory of it, its power as a weapon against the pathological denial of life.

AS: The book's title is 'Songs for the Devil and Death'. What sort of devil and death are you singing to, and why dedicate the book to these two?

HD: The devil? He's not some prince of darkness, that's for sure. Not the source of all evil, tempter and deceiver, punisher of sin, ruler of hell. Not even the tragic/heroic desolate rebel of Milton or Marilyn Manson. Though both are phases in the metamorphosis of the figure that lead to the devil I'm singing for, even the latter remains essentially dark, a symbol of our animal selves but one fetishistically glamoured with transgression – in an implicit equation of the animal with the bestial that surrenders the semiotic battlefield to the same old Jekyll-and-Hyde duality of spirit and flesh, mind and body, reason and passion, thought and instinct, man and beast.

I'm singing for the devil who renders such dichotomies null and void, the animal self that has abolished the demonisation of the libidinous id. My devil is the lightbringer who ordered the world and shaped us out of clay; who is on our side against the tyranny of neurosis enthroned behind the veil; who gave us the gift of ethical judgement as a tool to overcome that tyrant; who fell into night and fire because instead we crumbled in shame at our naked flesh; who was painted villain through an age

149

of crusades and inquisitions even as he drove us towards enlightenment; whose return was trumpeted in Nietszche's declaration, "God is dead"; who was, and is, and ever will be, the carnal impetus of animal humanity to sate the passions of empathy and curiosity that are every bit as instinctual as our brutality and disregard are <u>learned</u>.

The devil I sing for is the <u>daimon</u> of <u>eudaimonia</u>, the <u>theos</u> of <u>enthousiasmos</u>. He's known as Satan because that means literally "accuser" or "adversary." He's defined by his oppositional stance because he's the part of us that stands against even the highest authority imaginable and says to us, "Here is the capacity to judge right and wrong. Own it." He is the stance itself.

I reckon it's pretty self-explanatory why I dedicate my poetry to that devil.

As for Death, Aeschylus puts it best: "Alone of all the gods, Death has no love for gifts. Neither by sacrfice nor by libation can you bend his will. He has no altars and no hymns of praise. From him alone of all the daimons, Persuasion stands aloof." A god that can't be bribed is a god you can trust absolutely. There can be no privilege with Death, no preferential treatment. We all know where we stand, and we all stand in the same place. Death makes no deals; all you can do is <u>deal with him</u>... in that quite different sense of the term. Or in the Texas Hold 'Em sense, playing hands, pushing

150

chips back and forth across the baize, whiling away the hours in a game that will always end with him wiping you out. So it goes.

He's a capricious little bastard, my Death: "Jade eyes and autumn hair, a boy, he seems / to smile a truth of ivory and cream, / a grin of sin." Like love as a winged ephebe shooting arrows willy-nilly, he's arbitrary, disdaining all systems of valuation by which we might seek to barter, saying X doesn't deserve to die or Y deserves to live. He's as fickle in <u>when</u> he comes as he is faithful to the promise that he <u>will</u> come. But that caprice, in a way, makes him doubly reliable, renders him the foundation of the one value system with any real meaning: that any second might be our last makes all of them precious. People die. He taught me that, not the full import but... more than enough. It was a fucking hard lesson, but it's not like he was acting out of malice, simply on the turn of a card. So, for his impartiality, for the meaning he gives to life, and because he has no hymns to call his own, I thought it was time <u>someone</u> paid him a little respect.

Hence Songs for the Devil and Death. Is it horribly picky of me to note, as an aside, that it's singing "for" not "to"? The latter has a simpler meaning: that the works are addressed or dedicated to these two. The former allows a little extra nuance: one could also read it to mean these are songs <u>in support of</u>... or even that they're songs <u>on behalf of</u>.

AS: People who consider themselves advocates of modesty or those of the intensely faithful persuasion might criticize you for offering personal offense to their faith and to decency in general, seeing as how you make use of a rather expansive vocabulary and dare write <u>fuck</u> instead of <u>the f-word</u>; 'Wake' especially might suggest to readers that you have simply "lost your way" and are now angry, spreading foulness in blind wrath. What would you reply to that?

HD: Decency in general can kiss my arse. Propriety can go fuck itself. The arrant fucking insolence of those who presume to arbitrate our language, fencing off this word or that as "obscene," is an insult more profoundly overweening than any profane slur spat in the face of a cock-fluffing arsewipe. And it's not about my delicate sensibility being pricked by a slight. I find it <u>politically</u> and <u>spiritually</u> unconscionable—the perfectly fine principle of etiquette perverted to a cage of taboos one must accept in order not to be deemed "vulgar".

That the word "vulgar" was twisted from meaning "of the masses" to meaning "unsophisticated, unrefined" to meaning "crude, obscene" should be enough to expose the political ugliness

at play, the way this is about the petit-bourgeois turning the very language of the lower classes into a signifier of degeneracy – which is, of course, simply a way for them to invert, in their minds, the relationship of financial and ethical degradation, to see poverty as a product of depravity rather than crime as a result of deprivation. If calling it semiotic class war sounds hyperbolic, understand, I come from Scotland where that was a concerted colonial strategy with the whole language, not just the lexis of a class. Propriety in language is about privilege, power. "Penis" versus "prick" is the parlour versus the pub. That song sung in the bars and docks is sometimes bawdy. Deal with it.

And spiritually? To paraphrase William Burroughs, "I am not innarested in your condition." The notion that certain words for physical actions and organs – fuck, shit, arse, cock, cunt – are obscene is a pathological neurosis, as far as I'm concerned. If you have shame issues as regards your natural bodily functions, go see a therapist and abreact your trauma, don't foist it on the rest of us. If your cult's creed legitimises such shame with a disdain for the flesh in general and in particular for those aspects of it most prone to remind us that we <u>are</u> indeed flesh, this only makes your spirituality blasphemous. The flesh is sacred, cunts and cocks especially so; we're talking <u>life</u> here. That you assume the authority to denounce life is precisely why I call you out.

And trust me, this is not blind wrath. I have not "lost my way." I apply anger where it's fit, to the degree that is fit, like any good Aristotelian. It's called ethics.

AS: "Behold, from lies, the jaguar born." What is the jaguar?

HD: It's the necessary corrective, the anger where it's fit, ramped up to savage wrath in defiance of an unconscionable insult to the memory of the deceased, to <u>all</u> life indeed—the insult of a funeral ceremony which isn't just a harmless consolatory ritual but which actively <u>exploits</u> grief in order to bolster that life-denying pathology. I mean, platitudes offered as solace are touching from mourners who can't say anything adequate because nothing <u>is</u> adequate; but mouthed by a stranger in the valediction ritual itself that banality is an affront. Formulaic regurgitations of the deceased's personal history gleaned from a cursory interview or two with family, the details clicked into a trite spiel about how lovely the dearly departed was for X, Y and Z reasons – that's a fucking bad joke. But the way the assurances of afterlife pander to the rejection of grief, the yearning for it not be so, the impetus to bargain a way out, that's downright <u>malignant</u>. It's diminishing

152

the loss and facilitating denial.

Worse, predicate that afterlife on the acceptance of a particular ideology, and it becomes a sales pitch targeting the bereaved at their most vulnerable, aiming precisely at their weak spot: you can feel so much better if you just buy a ticket on the "flesh is fallen" train. Lead the bereaved through ritual assertions of not just belief in the afterlife but total unconditional submission to the One True God who grants entry, beseeching his mercy, praising his kindness, offering up the very soul of the dead to him and celebrating the certainty that it's going to a better place... then the entire ceremony is a travesty. That's diminishing the deceased's very life as a paltry preamble to the infinite rewards to be bestowed on them in the grave – and you too, of course, you too, if you submit – for being a good slave. Smothering the full import of the loss is bad enough, but capitalising on it to poison the appreciation of existence... that's beyond the pale.

The jaguar—image inherited from Ted Hughes's poem of that name, pacing fast in its cage, whirling from the bars, and on one level free "as the visionary in his cell," <u>incapable</u> of being truly confined—is the appropriate response of <u>fucking fury</u>. It's explicitly "false as all," because it's the form worn by the devil as we first find him in ourselves, bound in a bestial avatar of rebellion, prowling reveries of vengeance. If a reader sees only blind wrath in "Wake" I might also point them to this, say they've missed the recognition of illusion; I'm not writing this as that teenage kid, but over twenty years on, quite aware of the delirium of such fury. That's why it's not the vapidly dark black panther of full-on narcissistic rage, the compensatory fantasy of power that blind wrath would have written. Instead it's black and white and gold, complexly patterned. Like life, the libinous id, the carnal impetus of humanity.

AS: But surely you are misunderstanding the true meaning of religion? What about the consolation and comfort faith can offer? Isn't that better than sheer grief or an existence without god, and as such a useless existence?

HD: No, if that's the "true meaning" of religion, actually I seem to understand it better; I see the two assumptions there, and they're exactly what I'm arguing with.

First is a simple premise of emotional utility – that faith is not just harmless but practically beneficent, salving sorrow and boosting joy. This is an argument against the uber-rationalist Dawkins mob though, against someone arguing simply that faith is false, reason must cleave to the true, and that's that. But I'm arguing precisely that faith is not beneficial, that it's actively harmful. Looking at it just in terms of the self: it's suppressing grief that needs to be worked through; it's thwarting a natural process that not only heals but makes more hale, engenders a resilience to further sorrows and a deeper appreciation of joys; and it's fucking your values, devaluing life so as to diminish appreciation of joys, rendering the world bleaker, requiring deeper conviction for solace, fucking your values further... and so on, in a vicious circle. Hence pathological.

And that's even before we look to its impact on others. The pathology is often viral, seeking to spread its misery – propagation being a virtuous deed rewarded with pride – and it's often hostile, seeking to impose dogma – enforcement of values also being a virtuous deed rewarded with pride. It's arbitrarily hostile—enforcement is virtuous in and of itself, regardless of the nature of the dogma, which means you get the reward of pride for burning a sodomite, lynching a miscegenator, stoning a rape victim, anything as long as that's what the dogma decrees. And it resists reform – enforcement includes punishing dissent as heresy. Sorry, you can convince yourself that your dysfunction is emotionally advantageous for you and that makes it justifiable, but

153

the insanity is demonstrably dangerous, making that selfish lie ethically unconsconable.

The second assumption is a convoluted premise/argument of functional necessity – that existence with aims set only by motives lacks intrinsic purpose, that only intrinsic purpose is legitimate, that intrinsic purpose can only be invested by exterior agency, that the exterior agency can only be divine, that the divine can only be a "God," which is to say, an object of a particular theoretical class specified as existing with aims set only by motives. This is the cracked logic underlying the idea that existence has no meaning without God.

We're existential beings. We <u>are</u> motive – in the adjectival sense, producing motion, driving change. As agents, having agency, we are our own stances, that this is joyous, that is grievous. Loving, laughing, living, we have a whole fucking metaphysique of motives inspiring us in our engagement with the world, rendering it rich with meaning. If you cannot parse those motives into aims, from the simplest target to the grandest plan, that doesn't mean the rest of us can't. It's not hard to find a use for your existence; it's as easy as picking a stray dog from the pound and taking it home.

That second assumption is a cop-out. It's not enough, it says. It's never enough. But rather than seeing our

154

yearning for meaning as a natural hunger that needs regular satiation, it scorns the very instinct it should be listening to, insists that only the certainty of an ordained function gives us the capacity to find fulfillment. Only if we're a clockwork ballerina made to amuse our maker with mechanical pirouettes can we possibly fulfil ourselves by executing those elegant manouvers properly. A canny carpenter might suggest that one manouver we're made for is the adoption of stray dogs – <u>caritas</u> – but this is only legitimate, it's claimed, if his message is divine decree. And all of this utterly baseless because the imagined maker who has defined our use is cast as acting on the very thing we're rejecting as inadequate – existential agency, aims set by motives. Think it through, for Cock's sake: if meaning created in the action of choice lacks foundation, what the fuck use is it to found your philosophy on <u>meaning created in the action of choice</u>?

The life of faith is not an existence with purpose. That's a life with all meaning ripped out in the abrogation of agency, a life of empty motions in accordance with whatever writ has propagated itself through the pathology. And in so far as the certainty of ordained function serves to nullify the recurrent unease as aims achieved require new aims to be set, it's a life in which that hunger—the drive that makes us adopt stray dogs because we feel the need for purpose and are <u>fucking social animals</u>, born to care – is quashed. That's all you gain, the <u>loss</u> of the thirst that sings out when your agency requires exercise. And it is taken from you to the political profit of the faith's executives who maintain injustice by that writ.

Again, I say this is unconscionable. Where that song of passion makes the flesh a temple, to quote a jaguar of yore: you have made it into a den of thieves.

AS: You explain that the propagation of faith would be rewarded with pride, yet pride as such is condemned by many religions (certainly in Christianity where it ranks among the Seven Deadly Sins). Please explain what you mean by that.

HD: To propagate the faith is valued as a good act, and to carry out an act you deem good is its own reward, even if you see it as serving God. You've done what you should, answered the calling, chosen the path of righteousness; bully for you! You can call it grace, but this is just pride by another name. If it's not a fucking arrant hauteur transparent <u>as</u> pride to anyone not fucked up by that pathology – and it often is – this is simply because the self-satisfaction is offset by a baseline of abject shame so that the feeling of having done one's duty to God only alleviates the guilt and disgust, nudges it up to "humble" piety.

By Cunt, this pious humility is fucking <u>hubris</u> because it's pride blind to the fact it's pride, recognising neither the conceit in the conviction one is right nor the self-satisfaction gained by doing what you're sure is good. I dare say it's actually a strategy of the pathology to enable its spread by blinding the evangelist to the egotism of their action. Cock knows, if they were aware of it they might actually keep their egos in check; instead they just offset with shame so they have to spew <u>more</u> pious cant to achieve grace.

And yes, the faithful would likely deflect that I'm displaying that very egotism, railing from <u>my</u> pulpit. And yes, I'd say, but I have the fucking integrity to <u>acknowledge</u> the audacity and the pride of this, the rocks I'm navigating by. I'm not the one claiming humility on the one hand, and on the other that I know and do God's will. This would, in turn, likely lead to another deflection – that in admitting pride I'm admitting folly, that clearly if I think I can <u>use</u> pride without becoming a slave to it this conceit in itself is self-evident hubris. No, I say, no, it's called self-awareness.

With those Seven Deadly Sins – pride, envy, wrath, sloth, greed, gluttony, lust – and the seven virtues set as the rejection of them – humility, kindness, patience, diligence, generosity,

155

temperance, chastity – anyone familiar with Aristotle's notion of the Mean, the idea of virtue at a sweet point between a vice of excess and a vice of deficiency, looks at that and sees that it's just half the picture. It's easy to construct the other half, identify failures of character in deficiencies of the "vice," excesses of the "virtue" – shame, condescension, timidity, zeal, unction, austerity, mortification. If the Good Christian is set against the Wicked Heathen, the Good Heathen can be set against the Wicked Christian, virtues cast as the rejection of these hamartia – magnanimity, keenness, courage, poise, prudence, magnificence, ardour.

That's where it becomes about navigation, where the essentialist nonsense fails, conflating shame with pious humility and magnanimity with sinful pride. There's no integrity without the "pride" of self-respect, no inspiration without the "envy" of esteem for others, no valour without the "wrath" of fierce defiance, no equanimity without the "sloth" of tolerance. It's easy to see the folly of the greedy and the gluttonous, but it's just as easy to see the folly of unctuous and the austere. And if all our parents hadn't chosen lust over chastity, as ardour, we wouldn't fucking be here, any of us.

The point is that no emotional attitude is just plain wrong or just plain right; it's always a matter of context and 156 what's appropriate to it. Ethics is the navigational skill of judging that, striving for <u>arete</u>, excellence. Those crazy-ass dicta that humility is always better than pride, diligence always better than sloth, and so on? Funny how that evangelical hubris is reconstructed in the rhetoric of serving God <u>as</u> diligence. And how the sloth of uncritically following dogma is reconstructed as humility. One might almost think the pathology was evolved as a mechanism for reframing contextually unethical actions as intrinsically ethical, thereby facilitating the most heinous vice with spurious incontrovertable justifications.

But then you'd expect people to be aware of that on <u>some</u> level, feel <u>some</u> sort of incipient guilt and disgust at their base state of ethical spinelessness, an intuitive worry that they're weak of character even, prone to do any old thing that serves their selfish egoistic whims, regardless of its effect on others or on their own self-respect... a fear that they're susceptible to... temptation, I guess you could say...

Oh, wait a minute. That <u>does</u> sound familiar.

AS: 'Sons of the Law', your story in FU#4, is something of a gnostic-weird-western adventure. How did you come up with that gritty Western setting to tell that kind of story?

HD: The Wild West is the pre-eminent mythscape of the modern era. Superheroes may be touted as the demigods of today, but for my money the Western idiom has more archetypal stories. It was known as "horse opera" not just as an analogue to "soap opera" but because of the grandiosity. Shane is mythic. The Magnificent Seven is mythic. A Fistful of Dollars is mythic. Sergio Leone in particular understood the operatic aspect of the idiom; with his visuals and Ennio Morricone's music, there are scenes in his works that have the power of ancient ceremony – it's like watching some profound ritual play out before you, that three-way face-off between Clint Eastwood, Lee Van Cleef and Eli Wallach in The Good, the Bad and the Ugly.

Maybe it's the primality of the setting, in part: in the barren wilderness punctuated by tiny enclaves of towns, the frontier harks back to very origins of civilisation. It's a world sharply divided between the herder and the farmer, mapping directly to the Neolithic Middle East we see in Genesis – in Abraham's migrant herding, the settlements of Canaan. Every cattle baron is a Nimrod. Every wandering gunslinger is an angel in Sodom.

In the classic 50s-60s Western, it's pure heroism—John Wayne is Herakles, each movie a labour. But with the 70s Western, the mythic quality cuts loose and becomes something wilder, more ambiguous, even outright esoteric. Clint Eastwood is Dionysus in Thebes, the drifter come to town to bring down Pentheus, not an ideal man but a force of nature, a daimon. The Man With No Name has no name because he's something beyond such delimitation. That's why Shane becomes Pale Rider with Clint replacing the heroic ideal with a nameless preacher, a divine messenger, the title shouting his identification with Death himself. That's why we have the blatant mystery – in the ancient sense—of High Plains Drifter, in which he's returned from the dead to paint the town blood red, rename it "HELL", and wreak his righteous vengeance. It may not be <u>deliberately</u> mythic, may be just the dynamics of the discourse itself working themselves through, modern myths emerging naturally from the flux of ideas, but the depth of resonance is there.

Did Sam Raimi know that he was killing God on-screen in 1995, in The Quick and the Dead? I'm quite serious. Whether intentional or not, and however you rate it, that movie is a Gnostic mystery play in which <u>Redemption</u> is a town ruled over by a wicked king/judge, the demiurge <u>Herod</u> (Gene Hackman,) into which the golden-haired Sharon Stone comes as salvific representative of a <u>higher authority</u> – federal marshall versus local law – to overthrow the illegitimate tyrant. She's

157

Sophia, spirit of Wisdom, come to take down Yaldaboath/Jehovah. Leonardo Di Caprio is the tyrant's son, beloved of all, hope of salvation, Yeshua haloed in golden hair just like Sophia, his death scene a pieta where he sobs to the father who rejects him, has <u>forsaken</u> him, killed him. Out of Herod's own mouth we're told he's the Almighty, this is his town, his <u>world</u>: "If you live to see the dawn, it's because I allow it! I'm in charge of everything! I decide who lives or who dies!" And in this Christian mythos with the ethical values flipped, <u>of course</u> Russell Crowe is Herod's one-time <u>right-hand man</u>—his brightest angel, his captain of the heavenly host, his Lucifer – now turned against him, a pacifist, a <u>preacher</u>. I'm sure some will baulk at this interpretation, say I'm reading too much into it, but the religious references are direct bindings. It's the story of a battle to take back Redemption itself.

In 1888, Nietszche wrote, "God is dead." The Quick and the Dead is one story of how he died. "Sons of the Law" is another. I suspect with both it's less a case of deciding to tell that kind of story in that setting, more a matter of the discourse of the idiom itself offering up a modern myth because it's a figurative truth.

AS: I'm sure you are aware of a newly edited version of Mark Twain's 'The Adventures of Tom Sawyer,' one avoiding use of the "n-word" as is their eup

hemism for nigger or negro. Following the same logic use of these same words might make your story unfit for educational purposes or indeed a pleasurable reading experience, possibly more so since you should be acutely aware of the insulting quality of these words, such an editor might argue. What would you think/say of "n-word" edits to your work?

HD: I'd say that's bowdlerising and I don't believe in doing it for the classroom or for the drawing room. With the latter, I'm certainly not going to be happy with declawing for the sake of a cosier read. With the former, expurgate the text and it's not my story you're teaching – it's one that may have a totally different reading with that word expunged, that might even invert a key point by erasing or soft-pedalling a character's implicit attitude, which makes it an ethical issue. I apply the same reasoning I would with "faggot." If I put that in a character's mouth, it's likely there for a damn good reason, and if the story is worth teaching, it's in part because of that. I'd be happy to hear arguments on a case-by-case basis but my awareness of the rhetoric of abjection is why I employ it – to address it.

As an aside, I find it quite worrying with Twain, actually, for a different reason, because if you're teaching him at all you're going to <u>have</u> to face up to the racism, which is hardly just a matter of one word that can simply be changed to "slave" throughout, making it all A-OK. I just read "Tom Sawyer Abroad" a couple of weeks back, coincidentally, and the rendering of Jim is profoundly racist – a grossly infantilised stereotype. It's too long since I read "The Adventures of Tom Sawyer" itself for me to recall how he is in that, but if it's even remotely similar... I worry that this is actually a sop to white insecurity, that removing the flag which advertises the racism just makes it comfortably latent... for students and teachers as white as the editor, Gribben. Cause it's <u>fine</u> to teach now the racism isn't flagged, eh?

With my own work it's more that representation is not advocacy. If you're putting the word "nigger" in a character's mouth, you're rendering them as the sort of prejudiced person who uses that word. And whether they use it with utmost venom or casual obliviousness, as a bastard or a fool, it just means they're fucking racist either way, to be read and judged as such, and their words and deeds with them – those judgements to be mapped to such words and deeds in reality, past and present. Racism is a fact, casual racism included, and the acceptance of casual racism in certain contexts is something that <u>needs</u> to be rendered, in some ways even more than the blatant malevolence. It's all too easy to pretend that racism equals hate-spewing bigots, so <u>not</u> spewing bigoted hate equals <u>not</u> racist, but that just isn't so; that's a factor in current acceptance indeed, a way we elide the very idea that "decent folks" like us <u>could</u> be racist. This is where a story set in 1888 can reflect the contemporary blind spot by showing how the "decent folks" of then were oblivious to even the most flagrant racism. Never mind verisimilitude, it's about reminding readers that a fucked moral framework looks fine from the inside; you won't even think of yourself as being racist as you blithely treat people like shit.

The idea that "nigger" might function as a trigger word, that regardless of whether it's in a rendering of racist rhetoric or discussion of it as a word, just to see it on the page might offend an African-American reader... that's more to the point, but given the spread of opinion in that regard, the importance of tackling such subjects the best I can for me wins out over a caution I think would ultimately be playing it safe for my own benefit. Again, I apply the same reasoning I would with "faggot"; I'd want a straight writer of colour to exercise their integrity in its use, without self-censoring on the basis that

159

I might be outraged solely by its presence in the text. To be honest, I think treating it as a taboo would only empower the word rhetorically, make it a better weapon for the bigots.

AS: "I'll take the earth" you write in 'The Lucifer Cantos'. What are we looking at if/when Hal Duncan takes the Earth?

HD: You're looking at it now. Me and the devil – whose words those are in the poem – we've already taken the earth, not in a conquering sense but in a choice of allegiance. Which may even be the wrong word since it's not even a matter of picking sides there. In those last two cantos, with the deity fallen, it's a choice to abandon the cradle of pipe-dreamed eternity in an "exodus to holy flesh," a choice not to take the throne as conqueror, but rather to "embark for fields unknown," and it's not just mine or the devil's. The creche is left empty. "But angels hark now, all intone: / I'll take the earth."

All intone. Is that an exhortation for angels to listen, to join in the affirmation, or is it an assertion that they are all now doing so? You decide; it's your choice too.

AS: What can your readers hope for in the near future?

HD: There's a chapbook immanent from Small Beer Press – "The A-to-Z of the Fantastic City" – beautifully designed as you'd expect from them, and gorgeously illustrated by Eric Schaller. Part fiction-as-essay, part essay-as-fiction, it's twenty six entries on fantasticated cities, real or imagined, in many cases both. You'll find Ambergris and Viriconium in there, Dublin and Jerusalem, and some more exotic destinations – Further, Quiz, Zeropol. There's even an introduction by eminent academic Henry V. Duncan, foremost proponent of the new "geological methodology" in the literary cartography of Fantasia, for whom I conducted the fieldwork that follows.

There's also a deal for a short story collection with Lethe Press, but that's only just agreed and we haven't even begun to discuss the actual contents, so I'm not sure how near the near future is in that case.

AS: One question you have always secretly wanted an interviewer to ask you? And the answer to it, please?

HD: Oh, I know! Question (in a much-aggrieved tone): "What gives you the right to insult the faith of decent God-fearing people everywhere? Just who do you think you are?" Answer: "Well, my mother's name is Rosemary."

AS: Hal, thanks for the interview!

HD: Thank you for having me!

* http://notesfromthegeekshow.blog-spot.com/

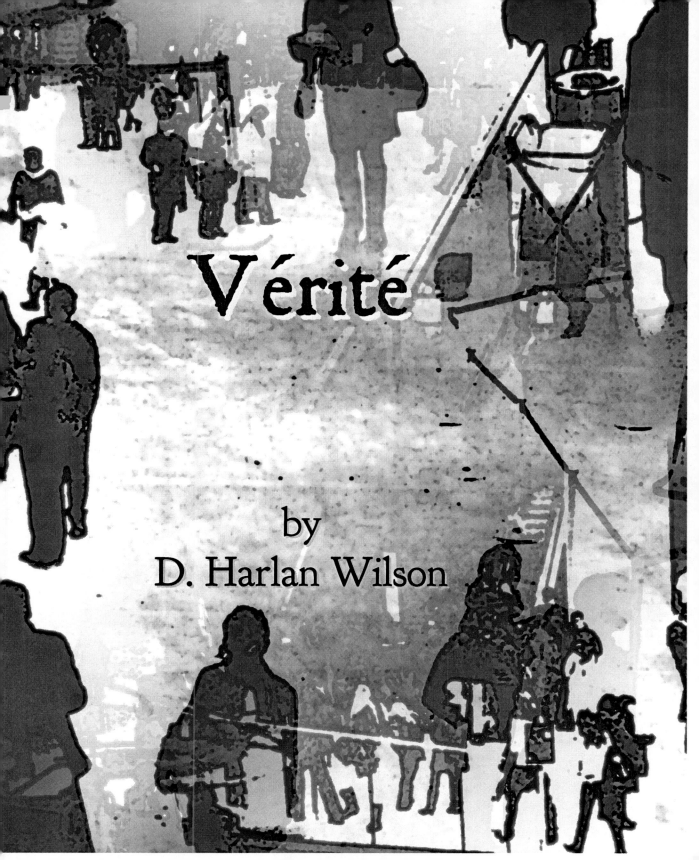

Vérité

by

D. Harlan Wilson

Herein, ignorance... or insight, art or artifice:

As I exited the movie theater, I recognized an actor from the film. He wore a stylish rubber jacket, pinstripes racing down the limbs, and the horns of dreadlocks had begun to form in his soiled, unwashed hair, especially around the ears. I knew his name but I couldn't think of it. He stepped past me and I said, "Weren't you just in that? The scene in the embroidery room. With Alistair Flank."

Arrested in a static blur, as if frozen by a pause button, he peered at me over his shoulder like I had sentenced him to death, eyes wide with alarm, chinskin twitching above a throttled neck . . .

"I'm sorry," I explained. But it was too late: I had implicated him by way of crude recognition.

. . . According to preordained estimates, the abduction process exceeded the combined span of the film's fight sequences. It unfolded in slow motion, and the actor disappeared into the sky on a beam of white noise.

In the parking garage, somebody had impaled my vehicle upon two great spikes, each of which rose at least fifteen feet from the concrete. I suspected a man named "Leete." I signaled a security guard and he brought me a ladder. The vehicle hung in the air like a sperm whale's severed head. I positioned the ladder at the rear, climbed it two rungs at a time and removed a mobile phone from the trunk. I dialed the first number that came to mind. Somebody answered, but the voice was incoherent and sounded more amphibious than human. Rearranging my grip on the carrying case, I gave the handset to the security guard and he spoke with the receiver at length about issues that eluded me; his tone oscillated between jubilation and dismay, and sometimes he fell silent, eyeballing me, and once he talked so quickly I couldn't make out the words.

"The situation is grave," said the guard, returning the handset. I put it to my ear but nobody was there.

"Grave how?"

"I don't know. That was the thesis of the conversation."

He tried to take the ladder away. I told him I would probably need it again. The scene drew a crowd. Steam hissed in soft curls from the undercarriage. Oil and antifreeze dribbled down the spikes. I spotted another actor and his celebrity wife near the elevator. He had not appeared in the movie, but he was no more than three degrees removed from it. I put the phone beneath the car and signaled them for a ride, calling out their names. Unhinged, they disappeared into a gaping elevator shaft, shrieking, as if yanked by a chain attached to their waists.

I asked the crowd to keep an eye on my things. I was slated to stand in as the lead singer for a local band, Pilots of Japan, whose frontman, my brother-in-law, David "Lady Strange" Smith, had contracted pneumonia. It was a serious affair. I needed to get to the plantation. The subway had stopped working last week. I would have to take a bus.

Time slipped away from me and I waited at the bus stop for hours. It was late now. All the shops and restaurants had closed for the night. In a different mind, I may have returned to the parking garage, retrieved my phone and made the necessary calls, but that seemed impractical, even dubious.

Heavy with fatigue, I walked away from the bus stop and the bus stop came loose from its foundation and tumbled upwards into an inverted funnel cloud.

In time, the scorched remains of a noonday glare incited memories of villains and the loss of causality.

A Slender Man approached me from what seemed like miles away, arms dragging across the pavement. I waited, even though the expression on his face, when I could finally read it, clearly specified a desire to incarcerate me. But he only asked for a cigarette. I gave him one, lit it, and lit a cigarette for myself. "I have no desire to meet anybody I admire," said the Slender Man,

---

"I have no desire to meet anybody I admire," said the Slender Man, exhaling. "I have done that before, many times, and they have always let me down. Admirable people should not allow themselves to be met. They should respect their talent and leave the world alone."

---

exhaling. "I have done that before, many times, and they have always let me down. Admirable people should not allow themselves to be met. They should respect their talent and leave the world alone." He took two quick puffs, made a face, and dropped the cigarette as if it had bitten him. "Disgusting. I despise smoking, and smokers. I am the greatest actor on earth. Thank you. Another version of myself will appear shortly."

"Me," I corrected.

In Oldtown, a blinking vacancy sign running vertically down the oxidized brick exterior of a hotel caught my attention. I had not slept in days. I had no way to get home. The steps came apart as I crept up them and the concierge welcomed me with festive rancor in the lobby. He was rough, gripping my arm and shaking me on the way to the room as he talked about disposable amenities and the continental breakfast that awaited me in the morning, sans croissant, regrettably. There were no lights in the stairway. I tripped, twice, and the concierge cursed and yanked me harder. By the time we got to the room, my shoulder ached, throbbed. It might have been dislocated. The concierge tore down the covers on the bed, gave me a complimentary bottle of Chivas Regal, and refused a tip. I never saw him again.

I drank until I passed out.

There was a knock at the door. "It's the concierge," said a voice.

I stumbled to the door and answered it and it was in fact the concierge. "This is no good," I slurred. "I'm not supposed to see you again." He began to shake me. I broke free of his grasp, tugged and jerked into my clothes, and fled the hotel.

From a rooftop, or a cloud, or deep space—another voice, cavernous and melodramatic: "The film you are about to see depicts violence and murder. Viewer discretion . . . IS ADVISED."

. . . Searching for the parking garage, I encountered my great grandfather, "S.R." He carried a stainless steel canister and artfully sprayed letters onto the front window of a pizza shop . . . A gas mask with a loud respirator concealed his jaws, and a snorkel ran down his chest and abdomen, but I knew it was him, the way he shifted and maneuvered his elbows, as if to remind me what it had been like to bounce on his lap as a toddler. He had been a successful artist, once, and a talented caretaker, despite the long cries of mourning that tainted his ancestry . . .

I tried to escape the attention of "S.R.", darting sideways across the street.

He detected me. He chased me.

"Cooper!" "S.R." cried out. It was the name of his wife, my great grandmother twice supplanted, and there was no mistaking us. "Cooper! I see you!" He sounded at once desperate, heartbroken, and happy.

I didn't look back. His voice dopplered into a virtual mist and then the cacophony of rush hour swallowed it. Bodies and vehicles and kiosks and cafés flew upwards, violently, against their will, against the laws of good cinema and acceptable alterities, stylized and staged for minor consumption . . .

The carrying case was gone, but not the phone. I stood beneath my vehicle and studied its underparts, a crisscrossing intricacy that most drivers never took the time, made the effort, or had the opportunity to take into consideration. I learned nothing.

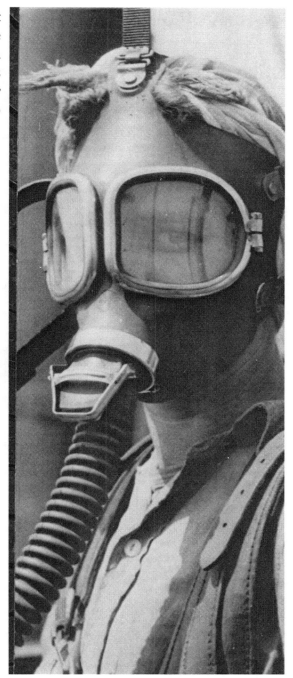

Seed the Earth, Burn the Sky
by
Mike Allen

The mountain god wakes,
stretches out his arms, laughs
a laugh to burn the timid moon,
and I explore the crags
of his torso with my hands,
trace the runnels of his belly,
the clefts of his chest,
the vales of his hips,
the secret, sacred pools boiling below.

The mountain god takes
my head in his hands, plunges
me in fire, holds me under till I melt,
crushes me into new shapes and
drags me up again,
and whatever form he molds me in
I dance
I dance as candleflame
I dance against his fingers
I dance to torch the pits of his eyes
I dance as he cremates me again

The mountain god scrapes
the sky with his wings, arches his neck,
bellows his echoes to me,
and every pale ghost I have ever held inside
swarms out, fountains up,
shades of baying beasts, of bone mutations
sacrificed to him in helpless cascade,
in a gale that shreds the air, howling as it rises
to rain upon the heavens,
to seed the sky.

The mountain god folds
(The morning bell sounds)
himself into the earth,
(The mourning bell tolls)
softens into loam,
(The morning bell accuses)
and I inhale his mud,
(The bell extols the end)
let him smother me beneath.
(of night, of breath, of spirit)
The day will never have me.

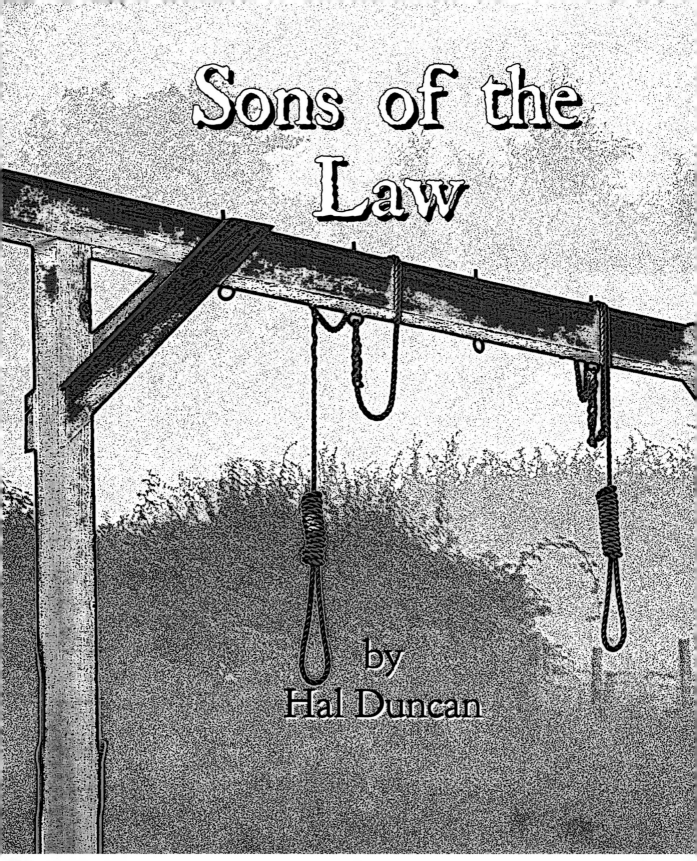

Sons of the Law

by

Hal Duncan

Herein, a reckoning...

The Legacy

The Wild West was born where fact ends and fantasy begins, in the elaborations and fabrications of journalists writing for the newspapers back east, in wild tales of gunslingers and gamblers that grew larger with each telling, written up as dimestore novels, as modern myths that some might call, in some ways, truer than the history. My maternal grandfather was one of those journalists. Between 1871 and 1882, while writing for the Arkham Herald, he penned a series of western novels under the byline of Randall Carter. They were never the most popular, so today even the most ardent bibliophile and historian of pulp might be forgiven for not recognising the nom-de-plume. No one, apparently, remembers his real name at all, not even within the family; strange, you might think, but so it goes. It was some Germanic sneeze of a monicker, they say, abandoned on his immigration. He was just plain Fred to

172

most folk that knew him, and these days, well, the truth of it is lost to history. Still, my uncle on my mother's side kept every one of Randall Carter's manuscripts until the day he died, whereupon they were passed to me, being the writer among us. My legacy.

Anyway, these manuscripts came down to me along with various notes and fragments, one of which, I noticed as I was looking through them, was headed up in bold block capitals with a phrase that caught my eye–SONS OF THE LAW. Reading on, I began to piece together the story of a gunfight that took place in an unnamed town, in an unnamed state, on an unspecified date, maybe sometime in 1882, best guess. Whether the interviews and scraps of description that make up the story have any grounding in reality or not, I don't know. It might be that my grandfather saw firsthand the bullets and the blood. On the other hand, it's entirely possible that what we have here are only notes for some fiction that he planned but, for some reason, abandoned. Whatever the case, I thought it was a story worth the telling and, out of respect, I thought I should let him tell it in his own words...

The Saloon

The saloon is quiet; you can tell there's something in the air. Trouble brewing.

The four strangers know that every eye in the place is on them, flicking from one to another, to the next, to the last, watching them all the time. For their part, they study each other across the saloon, silent and wary, like cougars meeting in the woods might circle to size each other up. Everyone knows these are the only players in the game–these four strangers and the Judge they're waiting for.

Standing at the middle of the bar is the hunter. His scuffed-brown, sand-scoured, leather overcoat well nigh touches the floor but at the bottom of it, sticking out, you can still see the tip of his Sharps Big 50, built to bring down buffalo. Though his face is shadowed by his hat, the grim steel-gray of his eyes catches the light. This is a man who's hunting for something, hunting *someone*, and everything about him says it isn't for the bounty.

Down at one end of the bar, clear space all round him, there's the killer. He has the sharp black waistcoat, black hat, black ribbon tie and rig–two Colt 45's in holsters, one each side, belted, buckled at the waist and tied around his thighs–that tells the world he's a pro. This is a gunslinger, with the cold heart of a rattlesnake and the deadly bite to match. Every man in the saloon knows his game, and near enough everyone can guess his name. At the moment, he has his eye on the hunter.

At a green baize table, back of the saloon, the gambler sits, dealing out a hand of solitaire and watching everything that goes on at the bar. Every so often, he brushes imaginary dust from off the shoulder of his immaculate gray jacket. From the red silk handkerchief in his breast pocket to the red silk cravat, he spells money. A lot of people in the bar are watching him, trying to figure out which way he'll fall in what's coming down. Nobody is sure. But you could lay good odds he has a Derringer up his sleeve and a jack-knife in his boot.

Last of all is the drifter, a young man–little more than a kid, really, sitting at a table on his own where he can watch the other three without too much of a trouble. He's less on edge than anyone in the saloon, so cool you'd almost say he didn't give a damn except for the way he's eyeing up the situation, like a big city theatre critic rating actors in a play. He's young, but he has old, old eyes. If you looked hard enough you might just be able to tell that the faded dusty outfit that he wears was once a uniform, stripped of all braid and all insignia. He tugs at the yellow bandanna around his neck.

The saloon is quiet, only the low murmur of a few hushed voices, a wrangler in the corner muttering to himself, and the strangled sobs of one of the showgirls to be heard–a pretty girl

173

in a dress all silks and frills, scarlet and purple. An old negro hums a sad tune to himself as he sweeps a broken bottle off the floor.

Over this, from outside, there comes the slow creak... creak... creak of wood under a swinging weight.

The Hunter

My pa, he was a farmhand for this big-shot land-owner, old army man, local Judge, real pillar of society. Tell the truth, I don't recall much of it on account of we left when my brother and me was still real young. Seems the Judge's son he kind of took a fancy to my ma and, well, he gave her an apple from the Judge's own orchard. She didn't want none of that boy though, she could see that he was mean as hell, so she takes the apple straight to my pa. Anyway, the Judge found out about it, there was accusations and arguments and the Judge he threw us all out. Whole family. You imagine that–on account of an apple.

Why, surely, Old Abraham's real proud to work for the Massuh, do anything for that man, slave or free. Sure and one day the Massuh he up'n asked me if I'd kill my own son for him. Yassuh, I said, I surely would, if the Massuh say so. And the Massuh, he says, Prove it.

Those were hard years, me and my brother growing up. That much I recall. We moved east and set up our own little farmstead. I'm telling you, we had nothing. The soil was dust. Every year praying for rain. You grow up hard. We put our blood and sweat into that land.

So, years later the Judge shows up, only by now he's moved on. Seems he's made himself a cattle-baron. His boy, he's split from him, gone off raising hell all over the state; shit, he's the meanest son of a bitch that ever lived, they're saying. Everybody's heard of him. Judge's son gone bad. And that just makes the old bastard meaner than hell.

So the Judge shows up and he's buying out land, raising taxes on the settlers, just cause he can, cause he's the Law, isn't he? And I don't know why, but my brother, my own brother, falls in with all his cowboys. He wants to ride out on the trail, wants to wear a gun at his side, wants a little excitement in his life.

Well, the Judge he wasn't happy till our barn was burned to the ground. Set fire to our crop, killed all our livestock. I

174

remember the smell of it to this day. My pa, he tried to stop me, but I went out after those boys, and you know what they did? They sent my brother back to stop me.

I shot him in a cornfield. I remember looking down at his body, and the blood just running into the earth. I knew it was him before I shot him; I just couldn't stop it. It'd gone too far.

Guess the Judge thought he'd broken me, cause he beat the tar out of me–Judge did, that is... wouldn't let anyone else touch me–and threw me in jail but they didn't hang me. No, they just branded me. That's where I got this here mark. They branded me and they ran me out of town. I told him then he ought to kill me. Told him then that if he didn't kill me, nothing would. I'd come after him and nothing was gonna get me till I'd finished with him. That's why I'm here. I don't give a damn what else is coming down, cause I know there's nothing can hurt me till I'm finished with my business. That's what this mark is. Unfinished business.

The Slave

Yassuh, I surely do love the Massuh. He's a hard man, but the Massuh he's always done right by Old Abraham. Old Abraham's been promised; Massuh he gone take care of Old Abraham's children, real good care. Old Abraham's gone have a hundred grandchildren, gonna be a whole nation someday.

Why, surely, Old Abraham's real proud to work for the Massuh, do anything for that man, slave or free. Sure and one day the Massuh he up'n asked me if I'd kill my own son for him. Yassuh, I said, I surely would, if the Massuh say so. And the Massuh, he says, Prove it.

Well, Old Abraham, he was sore afraid, but was he gone make the Massuh angry? No sir. Got more sense than to call for a whipping with his sass. Was he gone beg for his boy's life? Not Old Abraham. Not to the Massuh. So Abraham he takes his son up into the hills and he lays him down, would've killed him too, if the Massuh hadn't called a halt. Killed a goat instead. Oh, yes sir, Old Abraham learnt the Massuh's mercy that day.

But you see now? Old Abraham's gonna have a hundred grandchildren, and they gone be a whole nation. My boy he already started on that, and his littl'un, well, he's a fighter that boy, born free and like to wrestle with an angel if it got in his way. Might give uppity a whole new meaning, you mark my words. Some day.

What's that? Yassuh, he surely would've done. Old Abraham knows he would. Massuh, he lay down a judgement on his own son for being on the wrong side of the law. That's right,

175

that's the Massuh's son out there. His only son. Leastwise, his only proper son.

Surely. He was claiming to be a U.S. Marshall, he was. Massuh wouldn't stand for it. Townsfolk wouldn't stand for it, neither. Good folks round here. They knows the law. Yassuh, he's a hard man, the Massuh. But he's a righteous man.

You ain't never gone hear Old Abraham say otherwise.

The Killer

I love my father, surely I do, reckon in a lot of ways I only ever wanted to please him. But you know, he surely is a hard man to please. Nothing I ever did was right for him. I was always the proverbial bad penny, the bastard son he couldn't get rid of. Black sheep of the family. Reckon one day I just woke up and thought, to hell with it.

I say that. I say *I reckon*, but in honest truth I remember the day real well. It was the day I saw his true face, see, day I saw what he was really like.

He had this old slave, see, this old house nigger called Job, and one day he's cursing me and saying Job's a better man than I'll ever be, talking about how loyal and all Job is, and so on. Sure, I says to him, but what else has he got? Job, he's like a cowardly dog that no matter how many times you kick it, it keeps coming back, cause it's got

nowhere else to go and it's too scared to run away even if it had, and anyway it can't understand why you're kicking it. But you keep kicking that dog long enough and sooner or later it may just bite back.

Now, my father, my old man, he makes a bet with me, bets that no matter what I do, I can't turn Job away from him. Well, I was wild in those days. Hell, I burned in the night like the goddamn morning star. Now, I am not proud of it, I surely am not, but I took him up on that bet. Made that poor slave's life a living hell. And you know what? I lost.

That's when I knew. When I looked into my father's eyes, when he'd won, that's when I knew what power is, how it works. It's not fear. It's not being afraid of someone as gives them a hold over you. No, the kind of slavery I'm talking about, it don't come through chains and whippings. It's the kind that creeps into your heart when you're not looking, when all you want's a quiet life with someone else taking care of all the hangings and such that needs be done. That's where people like my father step in because they're bigger and heavier than anyone else, and they know, they know, that they were born to lay down the law. Power is in the knowing that you're going to win.

Every gunfight I go into, that's what I think. I know I'm going to win. Learned

176

that from my old man.

Now you may not believe me, but I tell you it is surely true that people have called me a cold and heartless son of a bitch. But that just is not so; mister, I am the goddamn fires of hell compared to my old man. Cold? You look into his eyes and, I tell you, it will freeze your heart. I seen him burn a town to ashes because he didn't approve of their fornication. I seen him blow a dam and flood a whole valley just to clear the settlers off it. I never thought he'd do this though...

You know, we ain't spoken to each other in about ten years; last time we spoke, know what he said to me? You were always my favourite. Looked me dead in the eye, face hard as stone, and said that to me...

I always knew he was a cold-hearted bastard, but I never thought he'd do this. I never thought he'd hang the boy.

The Showgirl

Mister, I don't feel much like talking right now, and I don't feel much like doing nothing else. I'm sorry, honey, but tonight, I just wanna get drunk. Well, sure, if you're offering. Ain't nothing in it for you though, mind. Bourbon, mister.

That's right. I knew him. Knew him better than anyone in the world, and he knew me the same way. He's the one man I ever met saw more than a cheap whore in a no-class saloon when he looked at me.

No, he didn't hurt nobody, mister. Wouldn't even wear a gun. I kept on telling him, kept saying that they wouldn't stand for it, that they'd come gunning for him. I think he knew it from the start.

Don't know if he was, mister. He said he was and I believed him. And he had the badge. But that didn't stop them, mister. That didn't stop them.

I know he loved me. First time I set eyes on him–when he rode into town with his boys and started tearing up the courtroom–the two of us just kind of saw each other as he was riding down the street. He was the first man ever looked at me that way, mister, first man didn't look at me like I was dirt. He looked at me like I was something special.

I think maybe we might have been married, you know? I think I would've liked that.

They ought to cut him down, though. Somebody ought to cut him down.

The Gambler

Yes sir, I sold him out, and I don't care who knows it. I'm a gambling man, son, and I surely do enjoy the living of my life on the dangerous side. Only sometimes Lady Luck deals you a

177

hand you can't do nothing with except fold.

Why, me and him, son, we went back a long way, but I tell you... there was a man who kept his cards close to his chest. Didn't give a thing away until that last game. I mean to say, I've played a lot of poker in my time, clean and dirty, and I never known a man so cool under pressure, not in all my days.

So we were playing cards, and that cheap slut, she's draped all over him like usual, of course. And all of a sudden he holds up his whisky and his cigar, and he says, You all gonna remember me when I'm gone, right? And he takes a slug of whisky and a puff on his cigar, and says, What you all gonna do without me? Well, all the boys start yammering about this and that, but I just sit there, quiet-like. I remember, I had aces and deuces, Dead Man's Hand. And while they're all yacking and yammering, he looks me straight in the eye and says, real low, You know, one of you boys sitting here is gonna sell me out. And I looked at the hand he dealt me, and I looked at him, and I knew.

I'm a gambling man, son, so I know a high-stakes game when I see one. And I looked into his eyes, and I knew he wasn't bluffing. I didn't believe it, but I knew he wasn't bluffing. Make it quick, he said. Make it quick.

Maybe he thought they wouldn't go through with it, but I don't think so; I think he knew the moment I left the table, he was a dead man. I think he knew exactly what he was dealing when he dealt me that Dead Man's Hand, and I think he knew exactly what he was dealing himself.

Times I think he was just tired of being the peacemaker, tired of having to carry the Law about with him, wearing the badge that nobody else would wear. But he wasn't a quitter. No, it's like he just decided that he had to die, that it was only when the people saw just how far it could go–just how much the Judge and his bought men were capable of–it was only then that they were going to wake up and see the Law for what it really is... and what it should be. That it was too heavy a weight for just one man to carry. We're all of us sons of the Law, he said once. All of us.

Oh, yeah. You like it? Real pretty piece of firepower, ain't she? Custom single-action Star revolver, silver-plated and engraved, ivory handle-grips. Shoots like a dream too. Cost me thirty silver dollars. I'm thinking she's gonna come in handy real soon.

The Wrangler

No sir, I never knew the man. Heard about him and all, but I–now that's a lie. I never ran with his crew in all my life, I swear. I'm just passing through, headed west. I'm telling you. I don't know the man, never have.

The Drifter

Well, I'm right pleased to meet you. My name... well... you can call me Thomas. Hell no, I'm just a drifter, travelling along, thought I'd stop off in this nice town for a drink and a bath. Yep, looks like something's going down here, and I don't know as I want to be a part of it. Rather just sit here on the sidelines and watch.

Now, it's funny you should say that, cause I spotted that too. Kinda spooky, don't you think, looking at some fella swinging on a scaffold and seeing a face as looks just a little too damn much like the one you see in the mirror? Kinda like someone walking over your grave. But, no, no, we ain't related or nothing.

Oh sure, I heard all about it, soon's I came into town. Sheriff damn near shit his pants when he saw me, looked at me like I was the living dead. I ain't surprised. Found out pretty quick why everyone was so jittery. Hell, I'd be jittery too, I saw the spitting image of a man I'd murdered riding down the street like a ghost on a white horse, while the dead body's still swinging on the gallows. But, as you can see, mister, I'm flesh and blood like you, and I can assure you that I'm no kin to that poor dead bastard out there. And if anyone's a–what did you call it?–*doppelganger*, well, you look a little closer, mister; I'd say, he looks just a tad younger than me. Stands to reason that makes it *him* that's *my* double, don't you think?

Maybe. Maybe it ain't such a good idea to stick around with everyone so edgy and all, and me looking like the dead man risen from the grave. But I'd kinda like to see how this all plays out. I don't like hangmen, see, and it might be nice to see this Judge get his. I got my reasons. Take a look at this.

That's right, me and the poor bastard on the rope out there share a little more than just our faces. This little neckerchief of a scar been with me for a long time now and I don't think it'll ever go away. They hung me too, my friend; they hung me and I lived. That doesn't go away.

It was back in the war, and some son of a bitch sergeant got me drunk and signed me up, see? Hell, I was just a boy, and I was never much of a fighter. I was scared. I ran away. Well, there was a Colonel–hardest bastard in the whole of the army–and he sent his men out to hunt me down. Wouldn't suffer no deserters from his troops. I ran for a long time, ran so long it seemed like all I'd ever done was run, but in the end they got me. Caught me in a cornfield, down in Two Rivers Valley, it was. Nowhere else to run. They got me and they brung me back.

179

I remember waking up in the slave-pen, waking up being dragged out of the slave-pen by the rope around my neck. Remember it? Hell, I dream it every night. Every night I dream I'm being dragged out of that slave-pen, up the scaffold to the noose. Every night I feel that noose tighten round my neck, and then the trap-door falls away and I'm dangling there, can't breath, except I can just breath cause it ain't on right and the weights are wrong which is why my neck ain't snapped, why I'm dangling there, and I can feel it digging in, and burning, and it's getting harder and harder to breath but, oh god, it takes so long to die, and I'm praying, won't somebody cut me down from here oh god forgive us all you bastards goddamn you all to hell. Every night I wake up dying.

Anyway, they cut me down too quick cause, with the weights and all, my neck should've broken and I should've been dead. But I wasn't. And they didn't think it right to hang me twice. That Colonel, he was thinking about it, you could see it in his face, but his daughter–Sophia, her name was–she talked him round. Still... I've never liked a man too keen on hanging, so I'm just gonna stick around here for a while, see what happens. This Judge, he seems to have made himself some enemies. I'd like to see... to see... that's him? That's him there?

God damn.

180

Outside The Saloon

The Judge turns and, without another word, walks out of the saloon and out into the middle of the street. He walks back to where the sheriff and his deputies are standing, seven men with a mercenary glint in their eyes, that greed for gold or glory, bought men, hired guns. He turns back. The saloon doors are still swinging.

The drifter comes out first, untying the yellow bandanna from around his neck. He wipes the palms of his hand with it, then winds it, wraps it tight around his left wrist. He flicks his hair back out of his eyes and takes up a position about halfway towards the centre of the street.

The hunter comes out and passes him, slowly, handing the kid the buffalo gun and a bandolier of ammunition, with a look that says he knows the kid can handle it, and walks on. How or why he carries such a weight around with him, you couldn't say, but as he takes his place towards the other side of the road he flicks back the leather flaps of his long dustcoat and brings out two-handed death: an eight-shot Le Matt revolver in his left hand–a specialist gun with a little single-shot shotgun barrel nestled underneath the main barrel; and in his right hand, a

Winchester carbine with a trigger-guard customised so that a flick of the wrist will twirl it round and cock it for firing from the hip in one swift move. Two bandoliers make an X across his chest.

The gambler strolls out, stops on the wooden porch of the saloon, leans on the support beam for a casual couple of seconds as he lights up a cheroot, then comes down the steps. He straightens his cravat, brushes at the brim of his hat and draws his right coat-tail back behind his holster. He stretches the fingers of his right hand out and curls them. He moves his left wrist slightly, just a touch, and there's an almost silent click.

The killer pauses halfway through the swing doors of the saloon to survey the scene: the Judge and his seven gunmen; the other three. He walks down the steps and shares a glance with the gambler that says, eight against four, good odds. He walks past the drifter, looking quizzically at the profile of the kid, then at the scaffold where the body has been cut down by the sobbing showgirl and some others. Cradled in the madam's arms, the dead man's head flops back. Same profile. They might've been twins.

The killer walks past the hunter, looking at the mark just visible under the shadow of his hat, the mark burned into his skin and deeper still. You can see it in the hunter's eyes, burning in his very soul. The killer walks on, walks right up to the edge of the scaffold and up the steps.

The showgirl looks up at him and he puts a hand on her shoulder. He crouches on his haunches at the body for a second, then stands up again and makes his way back down the steps. He strolls right out into the dead centre of the street, a little forward of the other three. Something glints in his hand.

The Judge swats at a fly that buzzes his face, flicking it out of the air with one finger.

For a second the killer just holds the glinting object that he's taken from the body of the murdered Marshall, then he pins it to his chest. The star shines silver in the sun.

Now we have ourselves a reckoning, he says.

And the gunfire thunders.

———————————————————

Fantastique Unfettered is one year old!

The thing that excites me about Fantastique Unfettered is all the talent that has united to create it. Despite my initial stumbling to reign in the tools and take an issue from conception to production, the talent of our contributors has always shone through. I see such improvements from issue one to now, but I hope you will buy those first three issues, because there is great stuff in those pages. The improvements will continue: I always see what is imperfect or lacking, which works a bit against my personal satisfaction, but drives that quest for refinement. We have big plans for 2012, including more Aether Age adventure (including the launch of the Aether Age eZine at www.aether-age.com and a very special end of year issue of Fantastique Unfettered that we are calling Shakespeare Unfettered. It will feature stories from left of center inspired by the bard (and by recent attempts to retell his works as homophobic screeds.) Whoa there, kimosabe. We got something for ya...

—Brandon H. Bell

FU is my very first editing gig. Needless to say, the zine and everyone involved will always hold a special place in my heart. I learned that editing ain't as easy as it seems, that it takes whole big chunks out of your day while you have to fit the day job in somewhere, and that I love it all the same. I even love the slush pile (for all non-writers, that's the stories and poems authors send in and that need to be read so we can figure out what to keep), in a way. It's also nice to know FU doesn't shy away from curse words or nudity (seriously! No pun intended), or anything else that some people might just label wrong. Happy Birthday Fantastique Unfettered! May people in one hundred years still speak and think of you.

—Alexandra Seidel

Georgina Bruce's stories have appeared in various anthologies and magazines.
Her website is www.georginabruce.com

D. Harlan Wilson is an award-winning novelist, short story writer, editor, literary critic, and English prof. His most recent works include two novels, Peckinpah: An Ultraviolent Romance and Codename Prague, and a fiction collection, They Had Goat Heads. Hundreds of his stories and essays have appeared in magazines, journals and anthologies throughout the world in several languages, and he is the editor-in-chief of The Dream People, a journal of anaphylactic texts.
Visit Wilson online at www.dharlanwilson.com and dharlanwilson.blogspot.com.

Carmen Lau currently lives in Berkeley, California. Links to more of her stories can be found on her blog:
http://carmenslittlefictions.wordpress.com/

Brenda Stokes Barron is a writer from southern California. Her fiction and poetry have appeared in Apex Magazine, Electric Velocipede, and Niteblade. She occasionally uses pen and paper to express sociopolitical frustration of which this story is a result.
Blog: http://digitalinkwell.wordpress.com
Twitter: digitalinkwell

Alma Alexander is an internationally published novelist, shorts tory writer and anthologist with work appearing in 14 languages worldwide; her novels include "Secrets of Jin Shei", "The Hidden Queen", "Changer of Days", and the newest one, "Midnight at Spanish Gardens". "River", an anthology of short stories edited by Alexander, is due out at the end of 2011. She lives in the Pacific Northwest with her husband and two presumptuous cats.
Website: www.AlmaAlexander.com
Blog: http://anghara.livejournal.com
Facebook page: https://www.facebook.com/pages/Alma-Alexander/67938071280
Twitter: @AlmaAlexander

J. C. Runolfson's work has appeared in Goblin Fruit, Mythic Delirium, and Stone Telling, among other venues. She has spent a good chunk of her life traveling the I-15 through Idaho, Utah, Nevada, and California, which was part of the inspiration for this poem. At the whim of the U. S. Navy, she currently resides in Florida.
http://seajules.livejournal.com.

Shweta Narayan was born in India and has lived in Malaysia, Saudi Arabia, the Netherlands, Scotland, and California. Her poetry can be found in places like Goblin Fruit, Stone Telling, and Strange Horizons, and her fiction in Strange Horizons, the Beastly Bride anthology, Steampunk II: Steampunk Reloaded and others. Her novelette

"Pishaach" was a 2011 Nebula Award nominee. Shweta was the Octavia E. Butler Memorial Scholarship recipient at the 2007 Clarion workshop.
http://shweta_narayan.livejournal.com

Lynne Jamneck is a transplanted South African living in Auckland, New Zealand. Short listed for the Sir Julius Vogel and Lambda Awards, she has published short fiction in various markets, including Jabberwocky Magazine, H.P. Lovecraft's Magazine of Horror, and Spicy Slipstream Stories. For Lethe Press, she edited the SF anthology, Periphery (available via Untreed Reads in 2011). Lynne is currently doing an MA in English Literature, unlocking the secrets to Edgar Allan Poe, H.P. Lovecraft, madness and the occult. She is writing her first speculative novel, a conglomerate thing of words featuring a lost protagonist and a city of secrets.
https://www.facebook.com/lynnejamneck
https://twitter.com/#!/lynnejamneck
http://lynnejamneck.tumblr.com/

Hal Duncan's debut VELLUM was published in 2005, garnering nominations for the Crawford, Locus, BFS and World Fantasy Award, and winning the Gaylactic Spectrum, Kurd Lasswitz and Tähtivaeltaja. He's since published the sequel INK, "Escape from Hell!", various short stories, and a poetry collection, SONGS FOR THE DEVIL AND DEATH. A member of the Glasgow SF Writer's Circle, and a columnist at Boomtron, he also wrote the lyrics for Aereogramme's "If You Love Me, You'd Destroy Me" and the musical, NOWHERE TOWN. Homophobic hatemail once dubbed him "THE.... Sodomite Hal Duncan!!" (sic) He's getting a t-shirt made up.
website: www.halduncan.com
Twitter: @Hal_Duncan

Jacqueline West's work has appeared in journals including Goblin Fruit, Sybil's Garage, Strange Horizons, and Ideomancer. She is also the author of The Books of Elsewhere, an award-winning fantasy series for young readers that debuted from Dial/Penguin in 2010.
www.jacquelinewest.com
www.thebooksofelsewhere.com
http://www.facebook.com/pages/Jacqueline-West/112573782122159?ref=sgm

---

Dan Campbell is most often at home in the middle of North Carolina with his wife and two daughters. His poetry has appeared in Stone Telling and Goblin Fruit, and his story 'Where Sea and Sky Kiss' is up at Daily Science Fiction. He is the poetry editor for Bull Spec.
http://art-ungulate.livejournal.com/

Kristine Ong Muslim is the author of several chapbooks, most recently Night Fish (Shoe Music Press/Elevated Books, 2011). Forthcoming books include We Bury the Landscape (Queen's Ferry Press), Grim Series (Popcorn Press), and Insomnia (Medulla Publishing). She has been nominated multiple times for the Pushcart Prize, Best of the Web 2011, and the Science Fiction Poetry Association's Rhysling Award. Her short fiction and poetry have appeared in hundreds of publications, including Abyss & Apex, Bete Noire Magazine, Expanded Horizons, Mixer, One Buck Horror, and Space & Time. Her publication history can be found here: http://kristinemuslim.weebly.com

---

Mike Allen works as the arts and culture columnist for the daily newspaper in Roanoke, Virginia, where he lives with his wife Anita, a goofy dog, and two mischievous cats. In his spare time he does a ridiculous number of things, including editing the critically-acclaimed anthology series Clockwork Phoenix and the long-running poetry journal Mythic Delirium. His own poetry has won the Rhysling Award three times, and his fiction has been nominated for the Nebula Award. His stories and verse have appeared recently in Nebula Awards Showcase 2009, Best Horror of the Year, Vol. 1, Cthulhu's Reign, Steam Powered: Lesbian Steampunk Stories, Strange Horizons , Apex Magazine and Stone Telling. Under the imprint of Mythic Delirium Books, he'll soon be releasing the Clockwork Phoenix anthologies for Kindle, as well as The Button Bin and Other Horrors, a collection of his best horror stories.

Homepage: http://descentintolight.com/
Livejournal: http://time-shark.livejournal.com/

188

Twitter: http://twitter.com/mythicdelirium
Facebook: https://www.facebook.com/time.shark

Kaolin Fire (http://www.erif.org/) is a conglomeration of ideas, side projects, and experiments. Outside of his primary occupation, he also programs open source games (http://www.erif.org/code/games/), edits Greatest Uncommon Denominator Magazine (http://www.gudmagazine.com), and occasionally teaches computer science. He has had short fiction published in Tuesday Shorts, Strange Horizons, Escape Velocity, and Alienskin Magazine, among others.

Twitter: @kaolinfire
Website: http://erif.org/

Luis Beltrán tells the stories of his daydreams through his latest body of digital print photographs. These quietly seductive works hold a deep and moving quality of innocent desire. Figures appear at the ends of alleys, above cityscapes, and up trees; they draw you towards them, making the eye chase its new companion. Beltrán's photos produce a dreamlike sensation, the product of their deeply saturated, yet muted, coloration. While objects around the periphery of the central image maintain a luscious intensity with their dark shadows and full mid-tones, the focus shifts as the eyes finds a hazy subconscious perspective. The figures which are central to this misty state call feel-

ingly to the viewer. Beltrán has created a world that captures a sense of the 'other,' and speaks to the mind's natural curiosity. His photos call to a place within us all and echo the inner child's adventurous and courageous nature. Luis Beltrán was born in Spain and still lives there, in Valencia.
www.luisbeltran.es

M. S. Corley is a freelance illustrator and graphic designer who is strongly influenced by literature and the past. He currently lives in Washington with his wife and cat named Dinah.
http://www.mscorley.blogspot.com/
http://www.flickr.com/photos/mscorley/
http://mscorley.deviantart.com/gallery/

Alexandra Seidel (Poetry Editor, Interviews, Reviews) Alexa has a powerful affection for the unreal and strange, the weird, the wicked, and naturally, the beautiful. She loves speculative writing because all these things come together there with the power to create universes. She is on board as an interviewer since Issue Two and joined the FU staff as "badass" poetry editor and reviewer soon after. She keeps random thoughts and a bibliography of her own work at her blog:
www.tigerinthematchstickbox.blogspot.com
You can also follow her on Twitter:
@Alexa_Seidel
(Review queries may be send to Alexa at poetry-editor@fantastique-unfettered.com)

Brandon H. Bell is the author of Elegant Threat, published in the M-Brane Double along with Alex Jeffer's The New People. He is co-editor of The Aether Age: Helios & managing/fiction editor of Fantastique Unfettered: A Periodical of Liberated Literature.

His work has appeared in publications from Hadley Rille and M-Brane SF, as well as zines such as Everyday Weirdness, Nossa Morte, and The Lovecraft Ezine.

He is an advocate for sensible copyright and Creative Commons licensing, a member of the Outer Alliance (supporting his GLBTQ counterparts in the genre community) and a Rissho Kosei-kai Buddhist.
google: +Brandon H. Bell
blog: http://www.nithska.blogspot.com

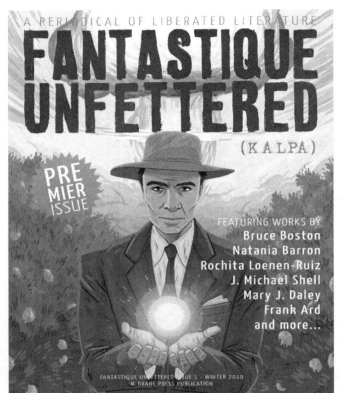

A PERIODICAL OF LIBERATED LITERATURE

FANTASTIQUE UNFETTERED
(KALPA)

PREMIER ISSUE

FEATURING WORKS BY
Bruce Boston
Natania Barron
Rochita Loenen-Ruiz
J. Michael Shell
Mary J. Daley
Frank Ard
and more...

FANTASTIQUE UNFETTERED ISSUE 1 · WINTER 2010
M-BRANE PRESS PUBLICATION

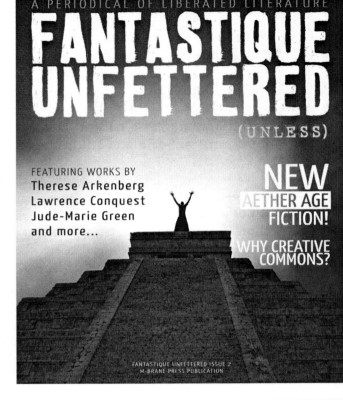

A PERIODICAL OF LIBERATED LITERATURE

FANTASTIQUE UNFETTERED
(UNLESS)

FEATURING WORKS BY
Therese Arkenberg
Lawrence Conquest
Jude-Marie Green
and more...

NEW
AETHER AGE
FICTION!

WHY CREATIVE
COMMONS?

FANTASTIQUE UNFETTERED ISSUE 2
M-BRANE PRESS PUBLICATION

A PERIODICAL OF LIBERATED LITERATURE

FANTASTIQUE UNFETTERED
(PROLEFEED)

INTERVIEWED
MIKE ALLEN

REVIEWED
HAL DUNCAN

FEATURING WORKS BY
Bruce Boston
Zen Cho
Sandra Odell
and more...

"the sensibility is 'literary,'
and the quality is high"
-The Future Fire

FANTASTIQUE UNFETTERED ISSUE 3
AN M-BRANE PRESS PUBLICATION

THE AETHER AGE

A PERIODICAL OF LIBERATED LITERATURE

FANTASTIQUE UNFETTERED

(SHIFGRETHOR

FEATURING
THERESE ARKENBERG'S
THE FOREST GODS

CPSIA information can be obtained at www.ICGtesting.com
Printed in the USA
LVOW051441080112

262862LV00004B/3/P